EVERYONE I LOVE IS DEAD

AMBER LEIGH LARRAIN

To all those who have supported my writing journey.
Every kind word has kept me going.

ALSO BY AMBER LEIGH LARRAIN

Psychological Thriller:

Blackout Girl

Until Death Does She Part

Cozy Fantasy:

Spellbound Beneath Sapphire Skies - Book 1

Spellbound Beneath Sapphire Skies - Book 2, Coming Fall 2026

ONE

Most of the moments in your life are inconsequential. It's hard to hear, I know.

All the little details that we obsess over—choosing to have coffee or tea, if you wear a red shirt or a purple one, if you spring for extra guacamole. None of it really matters.

Sure, while you are living it, it may feel important because we want to feel like each moment holds value, because then it means our life, our existence has value—but I won't remember which choice I made a week from now, and neither will you.

But some split-seconds can change the whole trajectory of one's life.

And for everyone around me, that moment was the second they met me.

March, 2024

5 years, 5 funerals.

I walked down the center aisle of the large church to my

awaiting seat in the front pew. The red carpet below my feet and the stained-glass windows flanking each side were the only sources of color in the sea of black suits and dresses. People reached for me, said things to me; I assumed condolences. Nothing registered. I floated along towards the front of the church, as if I were a ghost.

Despite each pew being filled, I felt like I was the only person left in the world. A loneliness and sadness so overwhelming I could physically feel it, like hands gripping my shoulders and pushing me down into the Earth, as if it wanted to bury me with my loved one.

The first pew was the only one that remained empty, waiting for me to fill it. The last piece needed in place to start the ceremony. Standing in front of my seat, I awkwardly adjusted the worn black dress I was wearing. I pulled at the hem several times, pretending to be fixing something, and then rolled my shoulders as if readying myself for an athletic event. This was happening. I couldn't stop it from happening no matter how much I tried to stall.

I settled into the hard wooden seat as my husband held my trembling hand. My heart skipped a beat. There was no warmth in his touch, but I smiled at having him there. He was a constant comfort in all the chaos that swirled around me.

Once seated, the organ that had been loudly playing Chopin's funeral march abruptly stopped. I was already overstimulated—this was too much. I felt like I couldn't handle it. I thought about moving to the back of the church, or better yet, running out of the whole building but knew I couldn't. I was stuck there. My place was front and center, where I must play the part everyone expected. Dab your eyes, have tears flow and stain your shirt, let your lip quiver. But those things were not happening, because my sadness was transforming into anger.

Behind me was everyone else. Overcome by my grief, they were nameless, faceless people.

I should be mourning the death of my loved one. But I couldn't. Because all I could think about was, who is doing this, why are they doing this and most importantly—who is next?

Two
Friday, March 13, 2020

That morning arrived softly. The sun's rays, like arms, stretched out to come through the blackout curtains. It added enough light to make me stir in bed. I arose when I felt ready, stretching with over exaggeration, then went to the kitchen to steal a quiet moment with my coffee mug. I picked up my phone and shot a quick text to the man I had just started dating two weeks ago.

> Want to grab breakfast this weekend?

I hit send and then added,

> Together.

When a reply didn't come immediately, I cursed my awkwardness.

Unlike most of my previous dates, we didn't meet on an app. We met at a local bookstore in mid-January when he approached me and asked if I had any book recommendations. I had to admit that I hadn't read a novel in a few years, but it was my New Year's resolution to read more. He laughed, and I was taken aback at first, thinking he was laughing at me, but then he admitted that was his reason for being there too. We ended up grabbing a coffee next door and exchanged numbers.

I recalled how he leaned in, over our warm drinks, and whispered, "I really shouldn't be here." I grimaced at him, assuming he was going to tell me he had a girlfriend...or worse, a wife. But then he said, "I actually own a coffee shop nearby. I'm drinking competitor coffee."

I lifted my latte and said, "To the competition." And he clinked his cup to mine.

His smile reached his eyes, creating little wrinkles, and I knew in that moment I was eager to see where this would go. Luckily, he invited me to grab coffee at his shop a week later.

About thirty minutes after my first text, my phone lit up with a response.

> Sure! Sounds great. Do you want to pick the place or should I?

I told him he could, and he picked one of my favorite spots in Collingswood. A good sign already! The morning continued to move gently, hiding the horrors that evening would bring.

Later that night, like she usually did, my best friend called. "Happy Friday the 13th," came Katie's raspy voice through the receiver.

"Good night for a scary movie," I replied.

"Britt, you know I hate scary movies."

Katie and I met in college. Despite the fact that I was going for a marketing degree and she was going for a degree in education, we had some overlapping classes the first year. Though our life paths began separating after that first year, our connection to each other never wavered.

We immediately clicked in a way I can't fully explain. If either one of us tells a joke, the other will always get it, meeting your punchline with hearty laughter or the perfect comeback. Meanwhile, everyone around us is trying to figure out what is so funny. When you find that person, the one who gets you on every level, as if you were designed to perfectly fit into each other's lives, you want to spend as much time with them as possible because they make you feel like a better, more alive version of yourself.

"You didn't come out with us last week," she said. It isn't accusatory, just stating a fact.

"I always feel awkward around your coworkers. They're nice but I have nothing to add to the conversation, and no one wants to hear about my latest advertising campaign. What can I say about lesson plans, behavioral management plans and big summer break trips? You know, some of us are a little jealous that we have to work every day for the rest of our lives."

She chuckled.

"Though I wish I could put some coworkers on a behavioral management plan. I'm working with this small clothing company now, and some of the influencers we are trying to collaborate with are seriously insufferable."

"Ugh. Sorry to hear that. Well, that's why you should have come out! We could teach you some strategies."

"I'll think about it for next time. Anyway, I had a date," I added. I knew this would pique her interest as I have had the worst dating history—though it has made for some good stories to laugh about later.

"Keep going..." she encouraged.

"His name is Ian. It was actually our second date, and we have a third one planned. So far, so good."

"Third date! And you are just mentioning this guy now? That's all you're going to tell me?"

"I don't know what else to say. We've had coffee together twice. Nice guy. Pretty cute."

"Oh...tell me more! Tall, dark and handsome?"

I laughed. "Brown hair, brown eyes, taller than me but no, I wouldn't call him tall. He's a few years older too. Is that enough info or should I get you his social security number too?"

"That will do for now," she replied.

"We're going out for breakfast this weekend. Can't recall the last time I liked someone enough for a third date. Should I start looking at wedding venues?" I heard her giggle on the other end. I propped the phone between my cheek and shoulder while grabbing the red wine I had chilling in the fridge. The scarlet liquid flowed into my mug, and then I tossed in a few ice cubes to make it extra chilly.

"I better be one of your bridesmaids! Remember I look terrible in orange and yellow."

"Noted."

"So, what does he do?"

"He owns a small chain of coffee shops in Philly. It's actually where we went on our last date. Pretty cool place. You should check it out." I pulled the phone away from my ear and texted her the link to his website. "I think there are two or three now, but he's thinking about opening one here in Cherry Hill."

"So, if it doesn't work out, at least you get a few free fancy lattes out of it."

I chuckled. "And maybe a scone. With my track record, that's probably the best outcome I can hope for. Hey, do you want to come over and watch a movie? *Pretty in Pink*? I've opened some wine. A merlot."

Katie snorted on the other end.

"What?" I questioned, already knowing what she would say.

"The way you drink red wine should be illegal."

Though she was a few miles away, I still tried to hide my smile. "I like what I like," I said, pretending to be offended. "So, no to the wine...but you can still come to watch a movie with me."

She didn't respond right away, as if she was considering the invitation.

"I don't know, Britt. Have you been watching the news? This Covid-19 thing seems serious. They are recommending we don't meet up with people yet. Until we know more about what is going on." I could hear she had the news on in the background, the familiar nightly newscaster's voice discussing the virus with a touch of uncertainty. "They had us write lesson plans for the next two weeks, 'just in case'."

"What does that mean, just in case? They can't close schools! Are the kids supposed to take your plans and teach themselves? That's absurd."

"I mean, they used two of our snow days to give us a long weekend. But what can that do? A disease spreading around the nation won't stop with a 4-day weekend. It might be a lot longer. Maybe a week or two."

"So, we aren't supposed to see anyone for two full weeks? That's crazy."

"It's scary, and I'm too young to die. I don't know what to think right now, but I want to take precautions until I know."

"Don't be dramatic. You aren't going to die! You're like the healthiest person I know. Maybe you'll get a little sick, that's all. But whatever! I guess I understand. I'll miss meeting up with you. Hopefully, this blows over soon."

"I hope so too, but honestly, I don't see how it could. From what they are saying on the news, it might be weeks. We can always FaceTime. Hey, hold on. I think someone is at my door."

I muttered, "Oh, so you'll let them in," but she didn't hear me.

I heard her footsteps, sticky like bare feet on a linoleum floor. The door creaked open.

Silence.

"Katie?"

More silence.

"Sorry, I thought I heard something at my door."

"What was it?"

"I don't know but it sounded like scratching at the door."

"Probably a stray cat."

She paused. "Maybe." But she definitely didn't sound convinced.

"Are you allowed to socialize with cats?" I quipped.

"Very funny," she said, but I heard her voice grow distant as if she was pulling the phone away.

"So...a socially distanced movie?" I asked again, but she didn't respond.

"Shit, I hear it again. Give me a second."

I moved toward the couch, wine mug in hand, the pieces of ice cubes clinking against the ceramic. I listened closely, waiting for her to finally let me know if we were going to watch *Pretty In Pink*. I specifically picked an 80's movie. It was our thing.

Honestly, I was getting a bit annoyed that she wouldn't meet up in person, but she's always been more cautious than me. Which was why I thought she was overreacting. *But who knows, maybe she isn't*, I thought to myself. *She does have her students to consider. Not to mention, this is uncharted territory for all of us.* I picked up the remote and began to scan Netflix for a different film. If she isn't going to join, I might as well pick something I'd prefer. Maybe I would watch a scary movie.

A loud thud made me pause. I opened my mouth to call out to her, but before the sound could come out, the shrillest scream I ever heard invaded my ear. I absolutely froze, fear shutting down my mind and muscles. The phone was locked to my cheek despite the horrifying sounds that continued to pierce my ears.

Katie's screams suddenly faded away and were replaced by repeated thwacking. Then all I heard were soft whimpers before stopping altogether.

All was quiet.

The whole time, I didn't move. I didn't speak. But my mind cruelly showed visuals for what I had been hearing. Tears involuntarily rolled down my cheeks as I sat stone still for what felt like hours, the phone still in my hand. I had disconnected it at some point but couldn't remember when. Then, a thunderous knocking at my door jolted me out of my haze.

"Police!" I heard a man shout, and I got up by some energy or force that did not feel like myself. This force opened the door and let them in. Looking back, it felt like I was outside my body, observing myself moving about but wasn't controlling its actions.

Two tall male detectives entered my small condo and sat across from me. They each had a face mask in their hands but didn't bother to put them on. It wouldn't have mattered if they were wearing them, though. I couldn't even describe them to you because I was staring into the distance the whole time, replaying my last conversation with her. In my visions, things were so different. I changed the ending—not freezing, doing something to help my friend, saving her from the attacker. Then all I saw was blackness.

"How did you know her?" the first one asked.

"What time did you first hear her being attacked?" asked the other one.

Then the questions kept coming. I didn't even look up to see who was addressing me. I stared down at my hands as I wrung them together. Focusing on that movement felt like the only thing that tethered me to my sanity.

"Who would want to hurt your friend?"

Once they got the info they needed from me, their facade of kindness was torn away, and they began to interrogate me as if I was the one who attacked her.

"You said she was your best friend. You look pretty relaxed right now. Are you upset?"

"How could you sit and listen to what happened to her? Wasn't that disturbing?"

"Did you have any issues with your friend that we should know about?"

"Why didn't you call the authorities? Or any medical help for her?"

My throat was tight, and I could barely get the words out. Finally, I looked up and asked my first question, "Is she...is she okay? Can I go see her? We might want to watch a movie tonight."

Both officers looked at me, baffled. They didn't respond for several moments.

"Brittany. I think you are in shock. I'm sorry to tell you this, but your friend, Katie, was brutally murdered this evening," one of them said flatly.

I lowered my head, and again my body shut down to the point where I didn't know if it would continue to breathe on its own. This was incomprehensible. My mind just couldn't process it.

Katie is fine. Katie is fine. I'll call her tomorrow. She will come over, tease me about putting ice into my red wine, ask me if I can hook her up with a free latte and then we will watch the Goonies. Or I'll even let her pick the movie. That will make her happy. She's fine. It's all fine.

"Ma'am?" one of them said, breaking me out of my delusions.

I looked up.

"Thank you for your time. We will be in touch if needed."

I showed them out and, in hindsight; it seems crazy, but I poured myself more wine and watched the movie I had planned to watch with her. It was days before I allowed myself to come to terms with what had happened.

A week later, dressed in a black button-down dress top and fuzzy Hello Kitty pajama bottoms, I attended her funeral via Zoom. A bottle of half-drunk beer sat behind the screen. It was my third or fourth for the day despite it being 10am. Sometimes I would lean sideways, out of the screen, and take a big swig. Many people said nice things about Katie through a few freezes and glitches. I zoned out, thinking about how she had worked so hard on two weeks' worth of lesson plans that were never used. I don't know why this part overwhelmed me so much, but hot tears slid down my cheeks thinking of those unopened documents. The last thing she did in her life had no value.

A text from Ian came in, and I held the phone out of view.

> How are you holding up? Just wanted to check in on you.

I typed several responses, deleted and started again. Finally, I settled on,

> I'm hanging on.

The breakfast date we planned never happened. I thought about asking him if he wanted to hang out that night but wasn't sure I felt comfortable enough to expose my grief to him. It was all still very new. I would message him again the next day and maybe set something up for next week when I would hopefully be in better shape.

I put the phone down and refocused on the Zoom service. With tears streaming down his face, her uncle talked about Katie, but either his or my reception was so poor that every other word was omitted.

"This is BS," I shouted, knowing she deserved better than this, and Zoom asked me if I wanted to unmute myself.

When it was over, I shut down the laptop and all of my emotions. I chugged the remainder of the beer, though it had grown lukewarm. It was all the same to me.

Later that night, I heard a knock at my door but I ignored it. I sat quietly, hoping they would go away, but they knocked again. Then I heard my name.

"Brittany! It's me. I'm just checking to see if you're okay." It was Ian with his deep voice, like a jazz singer.

I looked like hell but decided to let him in. We sat in silence most of the night, the hum of the appliances and my sniffles the only sounds in the room. I rested my head on his shoulder. It was the exact comfort I needed.

Right before he left, I grabbed his shoulder, and he turned to me. "Thank you. You have no idea how much this means to me."

He nodded solemnly. "Reach out when you're ready to go out again. We still need to have that third date." I looked down and he pushed a strand of hair behind my ear.

I told him I would, and then he was gone. The loneliness and grief invaded every part of my body to the point I wanted to crawl out of my own skin.

I sat on the couch, like I had the night she died, staring ahead but only seeing blackness. I understood it then. I was seeing the void she would leave in my life.

THREE

SATURDAY, MARCH 13, 2021

One full year without my best friend. Anniversaries are supposed to be celebrated, but the days leading up to the anniversary of Katie's death were making me jittery beyond belief. The void I felt a year ago did not get filled. Her absence in my life would be there forever.

What this grief journey would look like down the road was unclear. I didn't know if I would sink into a deep sadness or freeze up again. But today, I felt nothing, as if I was back in the moment when I heard it all happen.

A month ago, I had been called back to the advertising office full time and was thankful to not be virtually working anymore. Katie would have hated teaching virtually, but she would have done it well. She loved being around her 1st grade students. Each morning as they entered, they got to choose how they greeted each other, and most picked a hug, she would tell me with a smile on her face. I missed hearing her talk about her students and her class. Some of the things she would tell me they said were hilarious. She was one of the few people who really, really loved what they did.

It occurred to me what trauma her young students had to endure—the uncertainty of the pandemic at that time, suddenly being required to stay home, then finding out your teacher is gone and on top of that not even being able to comfort your classmates in person. I could picture parents saying things like, 'She's an angel now,' to try to help their little one process what happened.

The familiar sensation, eyes stinging, tensing up as my vision blurred hit me. No, I will not cry right now, I scolded myself.

"Keep on routine. Keep on routine," I repeated under my breath. My thought process was, if I could keep to my daily routine, I could keep calm enough to manage the day.

The last year behind the computer left me isolated and bored. Not to mention, another ten pounds (okay, maybe it was fifteen) found its way to my hips courtesy of stress eating and remaining cooped up within these four walls. Trying to deal with the grief during that time period only made the situation more complex, and I probably didn't deal with it in the healthiest of ways, according to my rewards points accrued at Dunkin' Donuts.

While working at home, I had more free time than when I had to go into the office, which meant more time for my mind to wander, and it frequently went to places I didn't want it to go. Dark places.

I often found myself at the keyboard, typing and then stopping mid-sentence, as that night played in my mind. So yes, I was thankful to be back in the building, with other people. It was eight hours a day of welcomed distraction. I could pretend to be normal, to be okay, when I was in the office.

My morning routine started to flow as it naturally did. The alarm sounded at 7:15am. I hit the snooze exactly two times and then got up, complaining it was too early. I got dressed for work, heated up the curling iron and wound strand by strand onto the hot stick until my dark brown hair was perfect, ran the mascara wand over my eyelashes quickly and then went to kiss my boyfriend goodbye.

I checked my watch. It was 8:20am. Right on time. *So far, so good*, I thought. *Just keep on this routine and I'll get through the day fine.*

Ian and I had been dating for a year, and he was a big source of support through my 'grief journey'. While we both had our own places, he often ended up staying over at my condo. The next step of moving in together was inevitably around the corner, I assumed.

"Brittany?" he said gently, grabbing my arm.

"Yeah?" I replied somewhat impatiently.

"Should we talk about it?"

I sighed and looked away, pretending to busy myself with a task. I ran the brush through my hair even though I had already done that once before. The loose curls had lost their bounce. "Not now."

"Tonight then?" Ian implored. "It's not healthy to keep it all bottled up."

"Yes, tonight. And I know, Ian. You say that all the time." I said with an exasperated sigh, mentally trying to figure out what I could do after work to avoid having a conversation I didn't want to have. Not today at least. Today needed to be like any other day, or I might shatter.

Maybe I'll stay late, have a 'project' come up. Ian always referred to the loss of Katie as being on a grief journey, and I can't tell you how much I hated that term. A journey is supposed to be a fun time of self-discovery. Sure, I'd learned some things—like how the oddest things can trigger your heartbreak, like passing by a restaurant you went to together, or how as soon as I felt I was about to cry I'd run to the bathroom so no one saw the tears. I'd learned things about myself, but I sure hadn't enjoyed it.

So yes, every time he said 'grief journey' I found myself wanting to lash out. To tell him to not say that stupid phrase ever again. But I knew he meant well, so I just bottled up my annoyance.

"Okay, well I'm going to head to work," he said, and then

kissed me on the forehead, and I felt the warmth even after he pulled away. "Want me to bring coffee to your office? On the house." He winked.

"No, that's okay."

His eyes lingered on me as if he was assessing if I was really okay.

Ian had derailed my routine. We never have serious conversations when I am getting ready to go to work. I grabbed my large blue tote bag and made a quick coffee in the instant coffee maker. All I needed was to maintain my routine and get through this damn day.

I checked my watch, 8:35am. Still on schedule. Coffee in hand, I started my car when my phone rang. My sister Melissa's smiling face filled up the screen, a photo taken from a trip to Wildwood last year. She was probably going to try to get me to talk about the significance of today too. No thanks. I cranked up the heat and pulled out of the driveway when the phone started to ring again. It rang a third time as I turned onto the main road.

"Jesus," I muttered aloud.

When it rang a fourth time, I clicked accept on the dashboard. "Mel, I can't ta—" The words were tumbling out of my mouth quickly, but I heard her sniffling and realized something wasn't right.

"Brittany," and her voice cracked through the speakers.

Immediately, I pulled the car over into the nearest parking lot, an overcrowded Wawa. It was like trying to play Tetris as I zig-zagged around the other cars in my effort to find a spot to park. I waited until I turned off the car before responding. "What's wrong?" I asked in a high-pitched voice and then held my breath for her response. She sobbed, breathing deeply as I braced for bad news. "What's wrong?" I repeated more forcefully.

"Mom. Dad."

"Melissa! Tell me what happened!" My hands gripped the wheel, but they were still trembling.

"They... they...." She stammered.

I tightened my grip and watched as the color drained from my knuckles until they were white as paper. I tried to channel my energy there so I wouldn't snap at her. "What? Tell me."

"They were in an accident. Oh, God!" she wailed.

"What hospital are they at? I'll meet you there." I could feel the blood quickly pumping through my veins, and it created a drumbeat in my ears. The repetitious sound only heightened my anxiety.

I heard her blow her nose and break into uncontrollable sobs again. She tried to get out words, but each was just stunted syllables. "Melissa, it's going to be okay," I said, trying to calm her so I could get the information I needed. In response, a sound so deep and guttural came from my sister that it cracked something inside of me.

She didn't need to say it. I knew they were dead. Katie. Now my parents. Exactly one year apart. I had already been trying to shove down all my emotions, but with this phone call, I could no longer do that. I sat in the parking lot trying to make sense of it all. How could this have happened exactly one year apart?

I texted Ian.

> I need you to come here right now.

Then, I shared my location.

Ian opened the passenger-side car door and he slid in beside me in slow motion. He acted as if any sudden movement could shatter me. "I know today is hard. Why don't you—"

"My parents died this morning."

He tilted his head, looking confused at first. "Oh, God, Brittany."

Not a single word was spoken after that. I just recalled melting into him while he embraced me. The emotions were so strong that I couldn't feel my own physical being. I was just the vessel for the emotions that were flowing through me, and he understood that as he held me.

"I never got to fix things with them," I said to him. Things were so deeply complicated with my parents and had been for nearly as long as I could remember. The regret was so deep that it felt as if it was tugging from my core to be let out. He made calming shushing sounds over and over. "I hadn't even called them in a week or two. I wish we had the chance to be closer. I did love them."

"I know that. They knew that, Brittany. Families are always complicated," he said, and I think I heard his voice crack.

I put my hand on top of his, and the touch instantaneously brought a bit of calm. "Thank you for being here for me."

"There's nowhere else I would be. I'll stay here with you as long as you like." And his eyes stayed on me.

A week later, I entered the Unitarian church that I had attended when I was a child. I scanned the room to see only a few other people seated. Their faces were covered by masks, so I couldn't even recognize some of them. It was a strange sight. Not one fitting of the full life they lived. In the back sat a camera to stream the service for those who couldn't make it. I took a seat, Ian on one side, Melissa on the other. I felt her hand slide into mine, interlocking our fingers, and I closed my eyes. For a moment, I could pretend to be somewhere else.

My heart clenched at the sight of such an empty service. They weren't perfect people, but they did make an impact on their community. They had been attending this church since we were kids. My parents deserved to have their lives honored by all the people they touched, but there were still many restrictions in place and most people still didn't feel comfortable being in large public spaces.

My sister, who was much closer to them, got up to give a speech as her hands visibly trembled, shaking the sheet of paper she read from. She said all the good things we say about people who have left us, leaving out the other side. Misdeeds are closed out with the shutting of the casket.

She doesn't know the things I know. These were two people whose ups and downs molded me into the person that I am today. Now they were gone. And I wondered if those attributes they instilled in me would vanish with them.

FOUR

Ian moved into my condo last month, and it's been a comfort that I didn't know I needed. Gone were the days of debating whose place to stay at, and I loved waking up with him beside me each morning. Though when I reached for him this morning, the bed was empty. I knew he was likely out running, so I propped myself up with my pillows, opened my book and waited for him to return.

Twenty minutes later, Ian came in from his morning run and pulled off his sweat-soaked shirt. I closed my book with a loud thud and glared at him. Today, I was determined to have my eyes on him and my sister the entire day, just to keep them safe. The fact that he was outside and alone annoyed me. I pressed my lips together, and he must have sensed my frustration.

"You okay?" he asked gently.

His deep brown eyes expressed so much love and concern, it broke down my wall of annoyance. I leaned in to kiss him, and his stubble scratched at my lips. "I wish you'd told me you were going out," I said.

"Britt, you know I run every morning now."

"Yeah, well, today isn't 'every morning.'" I twisted the engagement ring on my finger with its large pear-shaped diamond.

"Do you want to talk about it?" He sat next to me in the bed and put his hand on my thigh. I didn't mean to, but I pulled away. I just wasn't ready to talk about it. "I know that isn't really your thing, but you can tell me how you feel...if you want to."

He's been trying to get me to talk about it for as long as I can remember, and his persistence has been met with stone walling. I did not want to talk about it. I tried not to think about it, because if I did, I was worried I wouldn't recover.

The loss of my parents hit in a different way than when Katie passed. The issues we had will always remain unresolved and that was a difficult thing to process. You get into these thought cycles, a loop of your last conversation and you can't help but alter the memory, to make things different. Instead of being rushed to get off the phone, you take your time. Instead of feeling the frustrations boil in the background, you say, "Hey...can we talk about that thing?" And maybe you are able to work it out and finally get to a good place, leaving behind the anger and resentment.

Then you get pulled into reality and realize that will never happen. The wave of frustration that inevitably followed was as nagging as the perpetual drip on a leaking faucet.

I looked up at the ceiling, willing the tears to stay put. I couldn't cry, because I knew once I started, I wouldn't stop.

"Please, just talk to me. I know this must be very hard for you," he pleaded.

I said nothing and then went to get dressed.

He watched me as I slipped off my pajamas and I angled my body so he could see less of me. The weight gain from the pandemic never left and I felt so self conscious about my body. It didn't help that Ian had taken up running and now was more fit than when we first met. I tried to slip on an old pair of jeans, but I couldn't even get them over my rear end. It was mortifying and I let out a defeated sigh of exasperation.

"It's probably an old pair," he said.

"An old pair that I used to be able to fit into, Ian."

"It's alright," he said before I could slink away.

"Is it?" I snapped, looking down in disgust at the way my body looked in these too small jeans. "Do you even like girls this size? This isn't how I looked when we met. I'm worried I'm not your type anymore." My anger had morphed to self-pity.

He got up and came over to me. His finger guided my chin to look up at his face. "My type is you. Whatever you look like, whatever changes you make, or time makes, *you* are my type...always," he said with his deep voice, that always seemed to put me at ease.

I couldn't help but smile. I knew I'd never meet anyone as kind as this man before me. I cupped his face with my hands, feeling the rough texture of his stubble. "You are too good to me! But I have one more request."

"Yes?" he asked with a sheepish smile.

"I know Sundays are busy at the shop but I want you to call out of work today. I want you to stay with me, all day. Please, Ian."

He looked a bit surprised. "Britt, I know what you're thinking. It's natural to try to make connections but it was just a terrible, terrible coincidence. Everything will be okay."

I shook my head. I didn't believe that. Something was cursed about this day. "It's one day. Even if you don't believe me, even if you think it will make very little difference, can you please just stay home with me? If nothing more than to just be around if I need you. Consider it a 'family care' day."

Ian leaned over and kissed my forehead as he so often did. "You're right. I'll stay if it'll make you feel better—but listen to me, everything will be fine. I'm going to take a quick shower."

"Okay, I'll call my sister."

Ian grabbed a pink towel from the linen closet and went into the bathroom. I tapped my sister's name into the phone and then waited for her to pick up as I went to the window and peered outside.

"Hey."

"Hi, Mel. How are you doing today?" I immediately regretted asking it.

"Shitty. Can I come over?"

"No! No. I can come to you."

"Thank you. That's sweet. I just need to be with you today, ya know?" my sister said.

"I know, Sis. I'll be there in twenty minutes. Just stay there, okay?"

"Yeah. I'll just go grab coffee and I'll be home by the time you get back."

"No!" I practically shouted. "Ian and I will bring you coffee. Just stay home, okay?"

She reluctantly agreed and then told me she would text me her order. I was so focused on my plan for the day that I didn't even bemoan the fact that her order included so many extras that it would come to nearly $10. Luckily, I had my coffee connection.

I walked back toward Ian, who was drying himself off, noticing how toned and muscular his legs had become from running. "I know you are going to call out today but can we stop at Gritty Grinds? Melissa requested a latte with more directions than a piece of IKEA furniture."

"Being the owner has its perks—I can walk in while playing hooky and no one can say anything about it." Ian slipped on a Phillies t-shirt and grabbed his keys. "And ya know what? The latte is on the house," he said, winking at me.

Ian and I walked into the coffee shop where several people sat behind laptops, typing away. There was a young girl behind the counter who quickly slid her phone into her pocket upon seeing her boss.

"Hey Olivia. We just need to get a few things to go."

"Sure!" she responded cheerfully, probably thankful that she hadn't been reprimanded for using her phone.

He turned to me. "I'm going to go into the back and greet Mike." That was one of his partners in the business.

"Sure," I said, though I hated having him out of my sight. I turned to Olivia and read off my sister's complicated order and then ordered our usuals—a medium iced caramel latte and a large hot black coffee. When the orders were ready, I went to the back room and was surprised to see Charles, his other, more hands-off business partner was there too. "Hey Mike. Hey Charles. Haven't seen you in a while."

"Good to see you too, Brittany," said Charles.

Mike just greeted me with a wave.

I smiled and then turned to Ian. "You ready to go?" He stood and said goodbye.

With a tray filled with three cups of coffee, we knocked on Melissa's door.

"Hey sis. Hey Ian." Her voice was strained and her eyes were bloodshot, like little red spider webs. I set the drinks down on her coffee table. We all took our drinks out but no one seemed too interested in them.

The day went by in a blur. We mostly avoided the topic until evening fell and Melissa walked over to her bookcase. She pulled out a large brown picture album and Ian leaned in to whisper, "Do you two want some alone time?"

I shook my head, still set on having him right in my line of sight. She began to flip through and I closed my eyes, wishing I could escape this moment. When I reopened them, I was forced to interact with each memory and it felt like a herculean task. I felt Ian's hand cover mine.

The My Little Pony themed birthday party my mom threw for us when I was two and she was six, since our birthdays were close.

Our family trip to Hersheypark. Melissa standing next to me. She was four years older and towered over me.

A picture of us and some family friends at Long Beach Island, Anna and her family and Amanda and her family.

"That was a fun trip," I said, remembering bits and pieces of that vacation. What stuck out to my young mind was how amazing it was that we got ice cream practically every night.

Melissa wrapped her arm around me and brought me closer and I leaned in until my head rested on hers. Ian sat quietly, giving support by being there and giving us our space to grieve.

Once she had gone through everything, she put on our favorite show to watch together as a family—Friends.

We had been at her house for nearly twelve hours at this point, and it was clear she was nicely trying to encourage us to go home. If I left before the clock hit midnight, I'd go into a full-blown panic attack.

My sister yawned dramatically. "I've got work tomorrow and I think I better hit the sheets."

"Yeah, okay, but I want to finish this episode."

My sister glared at me suspiciously.

"It was mom's favorite episode," I fibbed knowing she'd relent at that comment.

Ian turned toward me and leaned in to whisper, "It will be okay if we leave." I gave him the death stare and he quietly said, "Okay, so we stay."

We hung around until the episode was over and then I tried to stall by cleaning up some of the dishes we left out.

It was 10:30pm by the time we arrived home and I knew I wouldn't be able to sleep until midnight hit. I took out my phone, hoping to find some mindless social media videos to distract me. Ian got in bed next to me and did the same.

Just then, our front door chimed and my fiancé and I stared at each other, unmoving. Slowly I started to shake my head as I whispered, "No, no, no."

Ian got up and moved around me very slowly, like how one would approach a wild animal. "There's nothing cursed about this day. Probably the neighbor telling us you left your headlights on or something." The bell chimed again and he yelled, "Coming."

"Ian, please," I begged.

"It's Melissa," he called back. My heart sank, misunderstanding what he meant, but then he flipped the phone around showing our doorbell camera.

"What the hell is she doing here?"

"I'll go find out," he replied.

He went ahead to get the door as I fumbled to find my robe. I walked down the small hallway and I could overhear their voices in the living room. My sister was saying something to Ian but I couldn't make it out. I walked into the room and he looked back at me with so much pity. "Melissa? Ian? What's happening?"

He ran his hand over his face. "Britt..."

"What the hell is going on?!"

"Sit down," they practically told me in unison. Melissa was twisting her blonde hair around her finger.

"Tell me what the hell is happening!" I was manic at that moment, wracking my brain for what could have possibly happened.

"I was scrolling on my phone before bed and saw something that you need to see."

Emotions and overwhelming thoughts were misfiring rapidly in my mind. She handed me her phone. It was open to a Facebook post from one of Melissa's high school friends, Leah Levitz.

My eyes darted around the page, trying to make sense of it.

We are heartbroken to say that my dear sister Amanda passed away earlier today...

Blackwood, NJ - Where I grew up.

Amanda Levitz - My grade school best friend.

Dead.

"How?" I asked after a few moments.

Melissa shrugged. "It was just an announcement. No details as to how. But there will be a service at the synagogue and then at the burial site. Will you come with me?"

I looked off to the side and said, "Yeah, of course."

. . .

We hadn't spoken in decades but when we were young, we were part of a trio. There wasn't anything we didn't do without each other. I recalled some of the times we spent together doing each other's hair, watching movies and riding our bikes...

"I didn't know who to protect. I didn't know." I wailed into Ian's chest. His hand rubbed my back in small circles.

"You couldn't have known. It's not your fault," I heard my sister say.

But it was my fault. All of this was my fault because everyone who passed was linked to me.

"Thanks for coming with me," Melissa said.

She had reconnected with Amanda's sister Leah a few years ago and I was there to support her. I felt it important for me to be there too. We hadn't been in contact in a long time, but she was an important part of my childhood.

We were standing in the cemetery, putting a rock on her tombstone. I caught a glimpse of her parents embracing and when her mother pulled away, her facial expression showed a level of raw anguish that I'd never seen up close. It was as if I was peeping into something too personal, yet I couldn't look away. Then her mother's eyes met mine and I quickly averted my gaze, embarrassed that I had been caught staring.

"We should go," I said to Melissa, walking as quickly as possible. She quickened her pace to catch up with me. As we dashed away towards the parking lot, hand in hand, I looked at her. "We have three hundred and sixty-three more days until this happens again."

She used her hand to pull me in closer, though she didn't respond. My sister knew nothing she could have said at that moment would have settled my anxiety.

FIVE

MONDAY, MARCH 13, 2023

My husband leaned over and kissed me on the forehead. "Good morning, Ms. Foster."

"Ian, you know today isn't going to be a good morning. A good anything."

He scrunched up his face. "Sorry, I was just trying to..." and his voice trailed off.

I knew I shouldn't have bitten his head off for greeting me but he also knew how anxious I had been lately. We had only been married five months, and I felt like he deserved the fun-loving girl who he first met, back when I wasn't always looking over my shoulder. That person was never coming back though, but I couldn't tell him that. I didn't want to lose him too.

Most days, I couldn't figure out why he stayed with me. Stress and anxiety were eating me alive. They were now my defining feature. How he could stand to be with someone so riddled with issues was beyond me. When he would try to soothe me, I'd get angry. When he tried to have a relaxing night at home together, I'd have panic attacks.

"Your sister will be here around nine or ten. We'll stay in today. It'll all be okay."

"People can die in the house too. Eighteen thousand people a year go to the hospital from furniture related injuries. Furniture! I don't know how to keep you both safe," I said, biting my lower lip.

Ian ran his fingers through my hair and I closed my eyes, focusing on the soothing sensation. I breathed in his scent—woodsy and musky. I could feel his breath on my ear as he spoke. "We'll stay safe today. Just don't toss a couch on top of me and we'll be fine."

I snorted. "Don't joke about it!"

Sitting at the kitchen table, I forced myself to slowly drink my coffee, focusing on the taste. I dumped too much of the vanilla creamer in so it was light and extra sweet.

I scrolled through my phone. Mixed along with my friends' posts, were sad news stories. I hadn't figured out how to block out those types of things so, being a glutton for punishment, I clicked on an article about the passing of an elderly couple. It caused me to tear up and I grabbed a napkin from the center of the table to soak up the tears. I used their grief as a replacement for my own. Then, I clicked away and texted my sister.

> Hey. See you at nine, right?

Five minutes. No response.

Ten minutes. No response. I drummed my fingers on the table.

> Please message back. Love you.

No response.

> Just text me back.

My hands were starting to tremble.

No response. One minute, two, five.

I started to type again when my phone rang.

"Can you please calm yourself down? I was in the shower. I know you are upset but we all still have to do basic stuff like eat and bathe."

I was so relieved that I didn't bother to argue. I didn't like that everyone was starting to get exasperated with me, instead of understanding why I was like this.

"Sorry," I said. "But you'll be here at nine?"

"Yeah. See you soon." Her words were quick and short.

"Make sure you turn on your tracking," I said, not realizing she had already disconnected. *Please drive safely*, I said over and over in my head.

I hated this day with such a fiery passion that it took every ounce of energy from me. "I'm going to lay down until my sister gets here," I called to Ian.

As I crawled under my covers, I closed my eyes and fell asleep almost immediately. When I woke it was 9:45am. I didn't even get out of the bed before I was calling for Ian. "Is Melissa here yet?"

"Nope, not yet."

I darted to the living room where he sat reading a sports magazine.

When he noticed the look of panic on my face, he closed the magazine and put it on the white marble coffee table. He tried to soothe me. "She said nine or ten. It's okay, Britt."

"No, Ian. When I spoke to her we agreed on nine am. She wouldn't be forty-five minutes late without telling me—especially today."

Then the doorbell rang. I looked at him like a deer in headlights.

"It's probably her. I'll go check. Just...just try to stay calm." Ian walked towards the door and I held my breath from the bedroom doorway.

"Sorry, I'm late."

As soon as I heard her voice, I exhaled, feeling the tension leave my body. I walked toward the living room.

"It's fine," he said tightly. He lowered his voice but I could still hear, "You know it's a hard day for her. She's on edge. Can you please text next time?"

"It's a hard day for me too, Ian," she snapped at him.

"I know but—" They both stopped talking as I walked into the room.

I forced a smile. It was so fake it hurt to plaster it onto my face. "It's okay! It's not a secret that I'm losing it."

They met my false smile with equally forced grins. We're all playing a part, though no one is convincing in their roles. Their eyes couldn't hide the pity they felt for me and I couldn't hide the low-level tremor that had taken over my body.

The two people I loved most spent the day treating me like a delicate structure that could crumble at any moment. They were right.

We passed the day dissociating on the couch and eating junk food. "What show should we watch?" Ian asked for the fifth or sixth time that day as he picked up the remote control.

We ran through a wide range of choices when I yelled at Ian that I didn't care what show we watched. He inhaled and then seemed to swallow down his irritation.

"Let's watch Friends," my sister said trying to break the tension.

"Great," I snapped. I noticed Ian and Melissa exchanging silent glances but decided to ignore it.

He put on the show and then put the remote down a little too hard and I jumped. My eyes watched the screen but my mind processed none of it. My only focus was to mentally calculate how long until midnight.

The room darkened slowly as the night crept in, casting a veil of secrecy over everything. Bad things happened at night. I slid my hands under my thighs to hide the fact that they were visibly shaking.

Melissa looked at her watch as she yawned. "It's nearly eleven pm. I have work tomorrow. I should go."

"Can you stay a little longer?"

She leaned over and kissed my cheek. "It's going to be okay. I'll call you first thing in the morning. And then maybe next year we can approach this day a little differently?"

"Yeah, sure. Fine," I mumbled.

"Text me when you're home. And once you get into bed."

She nodded as she grabbed her purse and keys off the end table.

Intrusive thoughts were telling me I couldn't let her go home alone.

Ian and I offered to follow her home in his car. As she got into her SUV I called out, "Drive the speed limit! Don't look at your phone."

She agreed mildly.

Ian drove and I played the part of the world's worst back seat driver until we pulled up to her house.

"I'm going to walk her to the door."

"I'll come too. I need to use the rest room."

Ian and I went inside her home and said good night.

Back at home, I got a text from my sister.

Good night, Sis.

Love you, Sis. Sleep well.

I stayed awake until midnight.

Ian snuggled up beside me. "It's over now."

As soon as the clock hit midnight, I closed my eyes. I had made it. Whatever had cursed me the past three years was broken. I could finally move on with my life.

I was awoken by the sound of banging on the front door at 1:32am. I cracked open the door and saw two men in uniform before me.

"We are looking to speak to Brittany Foster," said the taller man.

"This is she..." the words forming more like a question than a statement. I could hear Ian's footsteps coming closer to me.

"We are sorry to inform you that your sister..."

I recalled my legs giving out and Ian must have caught me. My whole world went black. No sounds, no sights.

They explained to me what happened but I couldn't process it. Suspected drug overdose.

"Was she involved in any other high-risk activities?"

"She wasn't involved in *any* high-risk activities," I shouted.

Ian put his hand on my back and rubbed.

"Melissa wasn't into drugs," Ian said, far more calmly.

"Do you think she could have intentionally hurt herself?"

I rolled my eyes and walked off into the kitchen. I needed to be alone so I could crumble into a puddle.

At the kitchen table, I covered my face with my hands, trying to block out this life that I couldn't believe was real. I left Ian with the detectives to answer all their questions.

———

One week later, we were at her funeral.

After the ceremony ended, we stepped out of the church, a sanctuary left behind us as we were plunged into a sea of flashing lights. I covered my eyes and asked, "What is all this?"

Ian took off his sports coat and tossed it over my head. "Fucking vultures."

I tried to ask what he meant but he couldn't hear me over the snapshots and reporters yelling questions at us.

"Why does this keep happening? What could have prevented this?"

"Who do you think is involved?"

"Have the police called you in for interrogation?"

Question after question was being lobbed at me as I hid under his coat.

When we got to the refuge that was our car I asked him, "Ian, what the hell was that?"

"It's the media." That's all he would say until we got to our condo. He focused on the road but I could see the tension on his face. I waited anxiously until we arrived at home.

After entering our place, he motioned for me to sit on the couch and he sat next to me, our legs touching. "That was the press."

"Yes, you said that before. But why? Why come to my sister's funeral? She wasn't anyone famous."

His eyes carried so much pain that I started crying before he even spoke. "They weren't there for Melissa. They were there for you."

"Me? What the hell? Why didn't you tell me?"

"Britt, I just heard late last night. Charles sent me a post that was going around on a local Facebook site. I didn't really think it would turn into anything, and God knows you didn't need more shit to deal with today."

I drew back. "What the hell did that post say?"

Six

WEDNESDAY, MARCH 13, 2024

The Proxy Black Widow. That's the nickname they use for me, mostly used in local social media groups but it was also mentioned in a few news articles. No one recognized me when I would go out, luckily, because I dyed my hair a soft shade of blonde and cut it into a bob. I looked nothing like the photo online. It's become somewhat of an urban legend though. A local woman who keeps losing people on the same day.

The police had briefly looked into it, and though I am the string that binds all these cases together, they have found that I had nothing to do with it. How could I? I wasn't near any of these murders when they happened. They asked us to hand over our phones, to see if we were in contact with anyone who was orchestrating it. We gladly handed them over to clear our names. The phones obviously came back clean. Other than that, the police had been very evasive.

"We're working on it," they said over and over without any evidence to show that they actually were doing much.

"We will call you when we have any updates." But they never did.

When I woke up that morning, I reached my hand across to the other side of the bed. It was cold and empty. Ian was gone. Rosco, our adopted six-year-old golden retriever, was gone too. Ian normally took him on a long walk each morning, trying to train him with better leash skills as he had a habit of practically pulling me to the ground when he saw a squirrel or rabbit.

I walked into the kitchen to find a note left on the gray marble island.

Walking Rosco. Be back in 30-45 minutes.
It'll all be okay.
Love, Ian.

Pain shoots up my arm as I aggressively slam the yellow post-it note down onto the cold surface. I couldn't believe he went out without giving me the chance to tell him to be careful, to stay home, all the things he knew I needed to say and do today. I called his phone and it went to voice mail. My wrist continued to throb, a reminder of my overreaction.

"Where are you?! You should've woken me up to come with you. Call me back ASAP."

Ian got this dog three months ago without asking me. Our grocery store was next door to a big pet store that was having an adoption event. He went out for milk and came back with a dog.

I was under the assumption we would pick out a dog together and that it would be a much, much smaller breed. It's not that I was opposed to dogs, but this one was huge. Sweet, but huge. Which means he took up a ton of time I just didn't have. Long walks multiple times a day, play time, trips to the dog park, taking care of him daily, vet visits. Not to mention we couldn't really travel with a large dog easily.

Despite the fact that, the dog was cute and mostly good

natured. I resented him to be honest. His golden hair was every-where. He had chewed through a few pairs of my shoes and now I had to store them in the bedroom closet. Ian seemed a lot happier to be around the dog than me, lately. Not to mention the walks seemed to be getting longer and longer, and I was wondering if that was for the dog's benefit or his. Was he trying to get away from me? Or get to someone else?

Over my morning coffee, I was growing furious. At the dog, at Ian, at both? I wasn't sure, but I felt hot anger bubbling up. I had left him a voicemail over fifteen minutes ago and no response. He knew he had to check in with me today. He should've waited until I was awake and we could have walked together, not that I ever actually walked the dog.

I quickly got dressed, slipped into my sneakers and looked up his location but it showed our home. "Shit," I said aloud, realizing he didn't take his phone with him. Normally he took the dog from our house to the high school, which was a two-mile walk there and back.

My feet hit the street and I ran faster than I ever had before, following his normal path. As soon as I found him, I wasn't going to let him out of my sight for the rest of the day. As I ran, I played in my mind what I would say to him, which only got me more worked up.

"We'll be together in a few minutes," I repeated.

I picked up my pace. When I got to the point where he would have doubled back, I looked around frantically at the large open field and saw nothing.

"Ian! Ian!" I frantically called out as I spun around. "Rosco? Ian!"

Hoping he was now home and I somehow missed him, I tried calling him over and over. There was no response. I called his phone for the fifth or sixth time and it went straight to voicemail. Why was his phone off?

My watch read 9:30am. I had been searching for nearly forty-five minutes up and down the path that ran along the field. If I didn't find him in the next fifteen minutes, I was going to call the police. Beyond the path there was a small hill that dipped down to a creek. Maybe he let Rosco get a drink? Or maybe Rosco pulled him and they tumbled down the hill? Maybe he's hurt. That seemed like a logical thing to me and I could feel my nerves start to settle a bit. *He probably hurt his ankle and I'll help him up and get him home.*

The sound of soft flowing water got louder as I approached the creek, eyes scanning the area. It took my mind far too long to understand what it was seeing and I stood still, trying to process it all. I saw what looked like a human body, a blob of fur beside him. I shook my head, hoping to reset the image, to see something new. But it was the same horrible scene. There he was, laying face down in the shallow water, Rosco calmly standing right beside him, softly crying as he nudged his side with his nose.

I screamed as I waded through the rocky water, droplets spraying everywhere with each unsteady step. I put my hands under his body and struggled to flip him over as I screamed out, "You can't leave me too!" Rosco tried to push his head under my arm and I pushed him away.

"Ian!!!! Ian!!!!" I knelt in the water, unbothered by the deeply cold temperature and placed his head on my lap. I yelled as I shook his shoulders, desperately trying to jostle him back to life. The calming sound of the babbling water was the soundtrack to the worst moment of my life.

"Please wake up! Please talk to me, Ian. I need you."

He never responded.

I looked up to the sky. "How could you take him too?" I screamed as I rocked myself back and fourth.

There were no tears in that moment. I'd honestly thought if I loved him hard enough, true enough, that we would be so strongly bound together that nothing could take him from me.

So many important moments get clouded over in your grief,

so I must have called 911 at some point, but I have no memory of it. When the paramedics came and told me he was gone, I knew whatever was causing this to happen year after year was stronger than any love.

It's been five years since this nightmare started, and now everyone I love is dead.

SEVEN

SATURDAY, MARCH 23, 2024

They suspected he had a heart attack while near the creek, fell in and drowned. We won't know for sure until the autopsy comes back but I already knew. There's absolutely zero chance that this was a natural occurrence or an accident. There was some evil lurking here and it claimed its final victim...unless I was next.

My seat was in the front pew. I passed all the people he impacted—friends from high school and college, people he worked with at the coffee shop and his regular customers, members from his bowling team Get Your Mind Out of the Gutter. He had some distant family in attendance but his grandmother, who he was closest to, the woman who raised him, passed away a few years ago.

I was wearing the same damn dress I wore to my sister's funeral and to my parents' funeral. You aren't supposed to get so much use out of this type of outfit but I didn't have the time or energy to get a new one.

Each row is filled, but it was all a blur to me. I didn't want to feel people's pitying, or suspicious eyes on me. I made my way to my seat, adjusted my dress and then sat down.

I stared ahead as the service went on. I closed my eyes and felt my husband's cold hand on mine. I opened my eyelids just a sliver and looked down, to see nothing there. I closed my eyes again. He's gone but I can still feel him with me.

Grief has hollowed me out and the void has been filled with rage. Anger at the injustice of it all. At the stupid things people say to you.

"He's in a better place now." Really? I think being home with me is a better place than in the ground.

"God has a plan." Really? His plan was to rip away the love of my life, so I could do what? Learn what a cold empty bed feels like?

Screw them and their stupid platitudes.

One would expect that I should give a speech today. Talk about how great Ian was, but I can't. I died with him. I was breathing, my heart was beating but everything else was completely shut down. My mind was often blank. My vision was fine, but I saw nothing anymore. The world was colorless, lifeless. My body was heavy as if it didn't want to move; content to just rot away.

Mike, his business partner, gave the eulogy. As soon as he was done speaking, I couldn't recall a word he said. I'm sure it was a lovely speech, and I probably even told him that after but grief does funny things to the mind. It was as if grief was a physical entity able to invade your thoughts and take up all the space so there was no room for anything else. I had hardly any memory of that day, despite its significance.

In my head, I gave the speech I couldn't bring myself to verbalize. That everyone here thought of Ian as a businessman. But he was so much more than that to me.

He was an architect, designing our lives to be loving and full of adventure.

He was an anthropologist, finding me, slowly picking away

the dirt, lovingly repairing all the cracks until I was restored into something valuable.

All those thoughts stayed with me. I said nothing aloud about him nor our life together.

No one sat next to me in the pew. Was it because they thought I caused this? What about the others? Or was it that I was seen as a dark cloud that could suck them into my misery, like if they spent time with me this would happen to them too? I was not sure what they thought of me and frankly, I didn't care. As soon as this was over, I planned to go home and figure out how I could join Ian...and my sister...and my parents...and my best friends.

Once the ceremony came to a close, I stood near the door as people said things at me. They weren't saying things *to* me, they were saying the things they felt needed to be said to a widow. It's more of a protocol than an effort to alleviate my pain. A way to make them feel as if they did their small part to help someone in distress.

I don't know what they said, probably stupid cliches. So, I responded to everyone the same. "Thanks for coming. It would mean a lot to Ian." By the time I was mid-way through the line, I'd lost all my energy and just muttered, "Thanks." By the end of the line, I was just nodding my head, often glancing at the door and counting down how many people are left until I could leave. Leave this place, leave this Earth.

Off to the side, I saw an older woman talking to someone about forty years her junior. Maybe it's her granddaughter. I didn't recognize either of them.

"It's like that movie I saw on TV last night. *Five Weddings and a Funeral.* Except this is the opposite."

"Shhhh!" she responded, frantically putting her pointer finger over her mouth. "And that's not even the title."

Senile old bat, I thought to myself.

The last person to greet me was a woman, tall and slender. I'd never seen her before and something about the way she was looking at me sparked something in me.

"I'm sorry for your loss," she said with sad, wet eyes.

"Thank you. How did you know Ian?"

She paused for too long. "We were friends."

I narrowed my eyes at her, trying to evaluate who this woman was, but this wasn't the place for an interrogation. "Well, I'm sure it would have meant a lot to Ian to have his good friend here."

She gave me a tight smile.

"You did a beautiful job planning the ceremony. Ian would've really appreciated all this."

"I think he would've preferred not flopping dead just when his life was getting started."

The shock on her face flashed briefly, but as I was the grieving widow, she gave me a pass.

I'd become a bit of an expert of the flow of grief and how those around you react to your situation. First two weeks, people are genuinely sympathetic and want to help you with tasks so you can focus on healing. I can't tell you how many casseroles I get in the first two weeks of someone's passing. First two months, people are 'okay' with your grief but aren't as eager to help anymore. The casseroles stop coming. They made you a lasagna a month ago after all so you should be fine. The texts to see how you are holding up stop coming too. First two years, they think, 'Why isn't she over it yet?' Not only do they stop asking about it, they really don't want to hear about it either.

As we are in the first two weeks, she let my off-the-cuff comment slide.

"I'm sorry. You're right." She lowered her head, clearly uncomfortable and shuffled out quickly.

When I got home, all the emotions I had bottled up, erupted. It was too much. All at once. I crumbled to the floor right in the entryway. Rosco covered me in warm, wet licks. I was frustrated with how oblivious he was. His owner, who loved him, was never coming home.

I pushed his head away from me. "How could you let him die? You could have pulled him out, you stu-" and then I stopped myself. I was angry as hell but I couldn't take it out on this dog, who loved Ian in return. They cherished each other so much during their short time together.

My life was like an intricate puzzle. In the beginning, it was all over the place and nothing fit. Just when we met, things were starting to improve. With his help, I put in the work and each of the puzzle pieces fit into place: husband, job, house, self-acceptance. I had it all. And then, once all those pieces were put into place, someone came in and with one swoop, knocked the whole thing off the table, breaking it all apart as if that work towards self-improvement had meant nothing. This was how I would remain—broken, shattered, unrecognizable.

I crawled into the bed and Rosco did the same, his body forming to mine. The warmth was like a security blanket. I nudged him away and he rose onto his four paws. However, he just circled a few times and then re-positioned himself where he was originally.

I pushed him away again. "You don't want to get too close to me. It hasn't ended well for anyone else."

He huffed out a breath as he resettled next to me. This dog was my only companion now. I flipped to my side and wrapped my arm around him. For the first time since I saw Ian, I cried. First it was a single tear, but then the dam broke. Huge tears dropped into his golden fur and he didn't seem to mind.

In the weeks after Ian's death, Rosco was my only tie to Ian. His friends and coworkers weren't in contact, finding it too difficult to be around me. I desperately wanted to be around those people in those weeks after the funeral. I wanted to be with someone who also missed him, so we could miss him together. Someone to understand how badly it hurt to lose someone so dear to me.

Trying to connect with his family was a dead end too. Ian was raised by his grandmother who passed away a few years back. He was one of those people who considered his close friends his family. And then, of course, he had me and Rosco.

So, despite the fact that I wasn't a dog person, never really wanted a dog, didn't care for them, I found myself growing attached to him. What I had seen as neediness and over the top energy, became a sign of love. When the thought occurred to me that this dog was my only friend, I thought for a moment that I loved him. And then I became terrified. I couldn't have anything happen to Rosco, my only connection to Ian, my only companion. Whatever I felt for this dog, needed to stay no more than basic tolerance—for his own safety. He was Ian's dog and I was taking care of him because there was no one else to care for him right now. My love was a death sentence and I wasn't going to fully give it to anyone ever again.

Rosco licked my face with his tongue, warm and rough. I smiled at him. "You're okay, Boy."

After the funeral, I was given two weeks off from work. I was told I could request more if needed. They said it like they were doing me a favor. As if having my entire future wiped out from me could be coped with and moved on in fourteen days, twenty-one if I asked nicely.

The first week was a blur. I didn't shower. I didn't get dressed. I probably ate something here or there but don't recall. I got calls and texts from coworkers and acquaintances but I didn't pick up. I was not adhering to any set schedule, and this was so foreign to me as I had always craved routine. Sleep happened at long stretches throughout the day and then very little during the cold, dark nights. The only thing that got me out of the house was Rosco's cries to go for a walk.

During the day I could busy myself with some distractions like doing laundry or reading a book but the nights were the worst. The cold and empty space in the bed beside me felt like an inescapable reality. It felt like looking at what could have been, should have been, taunting me.

Hanging on the wall was a vibrant painting, filled with pinks the color of soft blush and blues the color of the sky on a nice day. It's from our wedding where we hired a live painter to color a canvas depicting a moment from our wedding—our first dance. I looked over each detail—the flowers that will never wilt, the smiles of guests that will never fade and marveling at the celebration of love. There are the arms of the man I loved wrapped around my waist, leaning in as he said he'd love me forever.

Something in me snapped and without a thought, I took down the painting and smashed it repeatedly against the ground. The wooden frame cracked loudly but the canvas was still intact. I fetched a sharp knife from the kitchen and sliced through this moment that was supposed to capture our eternity. Nothing is eternal and to have it hanging on my wall was just a cold reminder of that. Some primal rage overtook me as I slashed through it over and over. Crimson blood smeared across the canvas. I felt no pain, but I had cut myself all the same. I ran into the bathroom to find something to wrap my wound.

Standing at the sink, I caught a glimpse of myself in the mirror. I let out a small yelp at my own reflection—never a good sign.

The shirt I wore, had been wearing for days, was covered in food stains. On a gaunt face, the wrinkles around my eyes looked deeper. My eyebrows were like two small caterpillars perched over each brown eye. My dyed blonde hair was growing out, exposing brown roots. I hadn't brushed it in days so it resembled a nest. I wasn't sure if it was fixable. Maybe I'd have to just chop it all off. I had a ghost-like complexion since I hadn't been getting any sun. Though my appearance shocked me, I still didn't have the energy or desire to do anything about it.

One thing was for sure, I wasn't ready to go back to work.

I called in and asked for the extension and to my surprise, they seemed much more accommodating than when they first told me about it.

"Sure! That's absolutely fine," my boss said over the line and quickly hung up.

Hopefully, by the end of the third week, I could manage to clean myself up a bit. I wasn't sure what next week would look like, would feel like. They say time heals all wounds, but I didn't see how that was possible. Each day would bring me further from the last moment we touched, talked, laughed. If that separation from our last moment was a rift, it would only grow deeper and wider as the days passed. The sound of his voice, the feel of his hand in mine, would blur and be left by a longing to experience them one last time, and that would be replaced by a longing just to remember those moments.

Each day would be a new discovery into who I was as this new person—this young woman who was a widow.

Thirty-four-years old and a widow.

A widow.

I'm a widow.

Though I understood it was true, it seemed impossible that this was my reality. So foreign that I felt like he had to walk through that door again at some point. He needed to come and sit with me, kiss me on the forehead as he always did, text me, 'about to leave work, want anything', let his stubble scratch my face. He couldn't actually be gone forever.

EIGHT

The day before I was about to go back to work, I felt exhausted. Somehow, doing nothing was draining all my energy. I just wanted to sleep all day and Rosco seemed content to follow the same schedule. He became my shadow. If I got up to go to the bathroom, he waited outside the door, sometimes waiting patiently, sometimes lightly clawing at the door as if knocking. If I got off the couch to get water, he followed me from the couch, to the cupboard, to the sink, and back to the couch. He wouldn't let me out of his sight and I wasn't sure if he was doing it for his benefit or mine.

Kneeling down to look him in the eye, I said, "I miss him too, Boy. But I won't leave you. You're safe with me." Rosco was all I had left. I worried he'd be next.

My phone rang and I saw it was from my work. I sat up a little straighter, trying to bring an ounce of professionalism back, as I sat in my grease-stained shirt. "Hello? Brittany speaking."

"Brittany. Hi. How are you?"

"Not great," I admitted.

"I can imagine."

"I don't think you can," I said, not hiding the disgust in my voice. "What did you need?" There was a brief silence.

"First, I want to say we appreciate everything you have done at the company. I wanted to let you know we had a meeting today, and several people voiced concerns about your returning."

"Concerns!"

I was so taken aback by this. I had worked at Next Days Advertising firm for twelve years. I was a model employee, having snagged our biggest account, an up-and-coming fashion designer. I created the ad campaign for a small cottage core clothing line. Their denim overalls with embroidered strawberries went viral last year and the small company's sales practically doubled overnight. Anyone who was anyone on Instagram took a picture of themselves in a strawberry field wearing them. The social media website had been flooded with copycat photos and many chose to invoke the Beatles with the caption 'strawberry fields forever', though the posters were far too young to be familiar with the band.

Anything you could ask of an employee, I did. Arrived on time each day, stayed late without complaints when needed. Spent way too many hours on social media to analyze where trends were going and to make connections. Always completed my work on time with the utmost care. I got along with everyone. Maybe that was the problem.

"What's going on?" I demanded.

"I don't really know how to say this."

"You're going to have to figure it out. You're telling me I'm not welcome at work, so I at least deserve to know why." I began to pace around the room, unable to sit still.

"Things just aren't working out right now."

"Like hell they aren't. What about Cartz clothing? They are going to want to continue to work with me." I ran my fingers through my hair. Was this conversation really happening?

"Cartz was the one who approached us first to have you removed from their account. It's an optics thing. They think..." He cleared his throat. I heard barely audible chatter behind him as if he had people listening in. "They are worried about the situations that surround you and the rest of the office agreed a separation was best. You know what they're saying about you, right? Brittany, they messaged me and were adamant that having someone deemed as a Black Widow wasn't in line with their cottage core image. You of all people should understand what's best for them."

I gasped. Of course, I knew what he was saying was right. But to think they actually all sat around to discuss this, to discuss me as if I was some cursed woman, to deem me unwelcome, was hard to comprehend.

"We can keep you on for another three weeks. You'd be working from home. But not on the Cartz account."

"How generous of you. You know what, at the next meeting please let everyone know that they can shove it...and that those denim overalls with the strawberries are hideous. They make thirty-year-old women look like toddlers."

I slammed down the phone, so enraged I hoped it would shatter the whole device so no one could ever call me again. I had no one, and now I had no job. No job meant no income. Paychecks would stop in three weeks. The realization made my throat flash hot and acidic.

Running to the bathroom, I flung myself over the toilet just in time to vomit. I sat holding onto the cold porcelain long after I stopped throwing up. The rancid smell assaulted my nose but I was too weak to go to another room. Running my fingers through the bathroom rug, I had never felt more alone and more pathetic. I heard Rosco softly wrapping his paw on the door. I ignored him so he began to bark. Crawling to the door, I let him in and he loyally took his place beside me.

Each day that passed, I felt more isolated, more sick, more exhausted. I couldn't find the energy to do much besides cry. My existence was starting to physically hurt. Looking back, it sounds crazy, but the voice in my head started to act like the friend that I needed.

"You should talk to someone," it said. "You aren't doing well. You aren't getting any better."

"I can't," I said to no one. "I don't even have the energy to pick up the phone."

"You do. It will be hard, but you can and will," the voice encouraged.

And so, I did, phone heavy in my hand. "Hi, my name is Brittany Foster. I'm already a patient there. I'd like to make an appointment for as soon as possible with Dr. Katz."

"Sure, what's the issue?" she said, with a slight southern accent.

How do I answer that question when literally everything was wrong, everything filled me with deep sadness or raging anger? I can't recall the last time I even felt a small spark of happiness. "I'm...sad," I croaked into the phone before I started sobbing uncontrollably. Lord, I couldn't get any lower than this.

"Shhh, shhh, shhh," she soothed. "You'll be alright. I'll get you in as soon as possible. Give me a second to get this ol' computer up and running, Okay?" Her accent, which was a pretty rare thing to hear around here, was calming.

I was a shell of myself. I had been right where I wanted to be in life before this all happened. Before I broke down, before I became a breathing corpse. I hear the clicking of the receptionist's keyboard as I thought about my former life. Everything I wanted was in place. A successful career and a husband who treated me well. I could afford the luxuries I wasn't able to as a kid—a nice car, travel and a handbag that cost way more than was reasonable.

Now, I was soon to be unemployed, had nothing but some funds from my parents' life insurance and an empty condo.

"Will tomorrow at three work for you?"

"Yeah, sure. That's fine."

"Ma'am?"

"Yes?"

"Will you be okay in the meantime?" She lowered her voice. "You aren't going to hurt yourself, right?"

"I doubt I have the energy to plan that." And I hung up the phone.

I suppose my answer wasn't convincing enough because within ten minutes there was a loud knock on my door which caused Rosco to bark wildly.

I propped open the door to see two officers standing on my doormat.

"Brittany?"

I nodded.

"We are here from the Cherry Hill Police Department. We just want to check in on you. Can we come in?" Asked the young woman. "We just wanted to stop by for a wellness check. Make sure you are doing okay," she said.

The warmth in her voice put me at ease right away. I motioned for them to enter and we all made our way to the couch. Rosco followed behind us, his nails clicking on the hardwood floor.

They sat with me for a while, assessing me like a specimen in a jar. Her and her partner sat across from me and Rosco. "Want to share with us what is going on?"

I smiled sadly as I petted the dog's golden fur. "You must know, right?" And they glanced at each other. "Well first my best friend died, and then my parents, and then a childhood friend, then my sister. And if that wasn't enough, my husband just passed away."

No amount of professionalism could hide the flash of surprise on their faces. They quickly composed themselves and began to ask me question after question in calm, melodic voices.

"I am going through a lot and I'm not handling it well, but I'm certainly not going to hurt myself. I barely have the energy to get up and shower most days."

I must have said all the things they wanted to hear because they got up and thanked me for my time. They felt they had made their final evaluation. All was as well as it could be, so they left. I almost wanted to call them back. It was nice having someone show interest in me, even for a few moments.

NINE

Rosco sat next to me on the couch, letting out long and high-pitched wails as he used his head to nudge me. When that didn't get me moving, he perched his legs on top of the counter and grabbed his leash in his mouth. Then he walked it over to me and opened his mouth, dropping the leash into my lap.

"Fine, but only because that was very smart of you." I touched my head to his. "Such a smart boy." He opened his mouth and it almost looked like he was smiling.

"I should compliment Ian on how well he trained you," I said.

Once the words left my mouth, it was as if they spun around and went straight towards piercing my heart. Though I knew he was gone, I often forgot what that fully meant and often thought of things I needed to tell him when I saw him, and then it would hit me.

I walked outside in my thin pajamas, forgetting how cool the spring nights were. "Just a quick one," I told him. Together we quickened our pace, hoping the movement might bring some warmth to our bodies, though his fur definitely gave him an advantage. We were nearly sprinting down the road when I saw a woman running towards us, decked out in pink from head to toe, her high ponytail bopping side to side with each step.

As she got closer, I thought I recognized her but couldn't place it. I didn't want her to know I was staring but it was driving me crazy. Where did I know her from?

"Brittany?" she asked as she pulled the headphones from her ears.

"Yeah? Yeah! Hi." Still no clue.

She paused in front of me and I could see she was wearing makeup. Who wore a full face of makeup while running at night?

She must have noticed the searching look on my face because she added. "It's me, Kelly, Ian's childhood friend. I introduced myself to you at the end of the funeral, but I can understand why you may not remember that."

"I actually don't remember much of it," I admitted and then crossed my arms, in a futile attempt to cover up what a mess I was.

The wheels in my head started turning. Ian had a childhood friend who lived close enough to be running in our neighborhood, yet I had never heard of her.

"Sorry. My mind is a bit foggy because of..." and I just let her fill in the blank, not wanting to put that into the air.

She nodded, understanding what I meant. "How are you holding up?"

I laughed. "This is hell and life is my punishment."

She looked away, uncomfortable, clearly unsure what to say to my candid answer.

"Where did you say you grew up again?" I asked to move the conversation away from me and to break the tension. She briefly flashed a questioning look and then corrected herself.

"Bordentown. Not too far from here."

"Ian didn't grow up in Bordentown. Not even close."

She shifted her weight from one foot to another. "Yeah, we were church friends."

I started calculating how long a drive that would be each

Sunday. Seemed very odd considering I could probably run past three churches on my way back home.

"And you live here now?" Rosco was growing impatient with our talk and started to pull on his leash. I patted his head to try to calm him.

"Yeah, a few streets over. I run a few miles each day so maybe I'll run into you again."

Show off. Why do people in good shape always have to let you know exactly how fit they are? Especially while I'm out here in an oversized t-shirt with pizza oil dotted all over it and my hair in a messy bun and not the cute kind.

"Okay, well it was nice to see you again. I better get going," I said.

I turned to walk away and she put her hand on my lower arm to stop me from going. It wasn't rough but just the shock of being touched, since I hadn't been touched in so long, made me freeze. It made me feel threatened, uncomfortable. Like I needed to get away from this woman right now.

Her face exuded kindness—maybe too much.

"I'm sorry?" I said, pulling my arm back.

"We both cared about Ian."

Did she? They apparently were friendly as kids but I hadn't heard of her in all the years I knew my husband.

"Maybe we could get together. Give each other support."

My eyes narrowed as I tried to size her up. "Sure, that'll be... fine." I said awkwardly and she laughed with her mouth shut, so it sounded more like a burp.

"So, when are you free?"

"I don't have much going on right now. Anytime is fine. I'm just over there on-"

"Lincoln Drive."

I nodded, but inside a flood of heat waved over me from head to toe. How did she know where I lived? After exchanging numbers, we parted ways with the promise to make plans at some point, a sign that we would probably never speak again.

I didn't know who this Barbie lookalike was or how she actually knew Ian. But what I did know was that I was going through my dead husband's phone as soon as I got back home.

TEN

Upon entering my home, I immediately double locked the door behind me and then let Rosco off his leash. Though he had freedom to roam now, he stayed by me.

I slid my hands through my hair and hit a huge knot. I ran into this gorgeous woman and I didn't even have my hair brushed. This gorgeous woman who had some mysterious relationship with my husband.

The world seemed to tilt. What if everything I thought about my husband was wrong? She seemed too familiar with him. I needed a best friend right now. Katie would have known what to do. A best friend to talk me off the ledge I was on, tell me I was acting crazy, that Ian loved and adored me and definitely wasn't seeing this woman on the side.

I placed my hand on the wall to steady myself. These walls that had seen our relationship grow from casual dating, to being in a relationship, engagement and then to marriage. Now there was death and loneliness. But somehow holding onto these walls made me feel calmer. Like the energy of our relationship was still within them.

When the destabilizing grief subsided, I went to find my husband's phone. Ian's phone was dead. So, I rummaged through his nightstand to see if I could find the charger. He always insisted on getting an Android while I always had an iPhone. I could barely figure out how to use his device, so trying to uncover any possible secrets the phone held might be impossible.

My fingers tapped in the familiar passcode. Our anniversary. The image vibrated and said wrong code. My trembling fingers seemed larger than the icons. I told myself I must have clicked the wrong numbers. Slower this time, I tried again, carefully landing in the middle of each icon. The phone vibrated again. Confusion sunk in. Why couldn't I get into his phone? The worries I had were only multiplying each time I was denied access. After several failed attempts, the phone wouldn't allow me to try again for several minutes. "Damn it!" I said and tossed the device into the nightstand drawer.

I pulled back the covers and tried to go to bed. Tossing and turning, I kept thinking about the past five years. Those thoughts made it impossible to sleep, so I sat up in bed, letting the images of our evolving relationship play over and over. I wasn't sure if I was going mad or if this is what people do when they have lost someone.

Two things kept nagging at me and keeping me awake. If he hadn't been cheating, then who was this lady and why was she so eager to get close to me? If he had been cheating with her, what was she after now that he was gone?

The sun was rising over the horizon as my eyes became too heavy to keep open so I finally pushed those thoughts away. I needed sleep so desperately that my body was physically screaming for it. So, I closed my eyes and drifted off.

My alarm signaled that it was 10:00am and time to get going for the appointment. I struggled to get up. The weight of the past anchored me to the bed. My stomach clenched as nausea seemed to rocket from my stomach to my throat. I ran to the bathroom and didn't make it, heaving onto the hallway floor. As I stared at the mess, I realized there was no one to help me when I was sick. There's no one left and everything I did from here on out, I would need to do on my own. As disgusting as it was, I couldn't bring myself to clean it up, not feeling like this. So, I left it there, along with all the other debris around my house. It would have to wait until my stomach settled.

Sick as a dog, I got myself dressed and into the car for my doctor's appointment. Driving in silence, I prayed they could give me some anti-nausea medication because while I was prepared to do a lot on my own, cleaning up my grief vomit was not one of them.

I waited in the light yellow room for several minutes before there was a soft tapping at the door. Dr. Katz, who I'd been seeing since I was nineteen, entered and greeted me warmly.

She sat down across from me so we were level with each other. Her eyes were fixed on mine and I squirmed a bit. I just wanted my prescription and to get out of there.

"You've been through a lot, Brittany."

I laughed. There was nothing funny about the situation but her words didn't even scratch the surface of what I was experiencing. She jerked back a bit at my laughter and I blurted out, "I just need some anti-nausea medication...and maybe some Xanax." I just thought of that as I said it, but it would definitely help. "A full bottle of Xanax...with a few refills."

She looked down at the clipboard in her hand and flipped through the pages. "We are going to run some standard tests before we can prescribe you anything. I still need to do your physical and ask some questions."

I tried not to roll my eyes. "Fine." I wasn't sure why I thought I could just get a few bottles of happy pills by just waltzing in here and asking for them.

"What symptoms are you experiencing?" She clicked her pen and then looked up at me.

"I'm tired. All the time. But I also can't really sleep very well. Sometimes I stay up all night and fall asleep in the morning. My routine is completely ruined. I'm not sure if it's depression or stress or both or something else entirely." She took notes as I spoke. I knew I was rambling but once I started talking, I couldn't help but continue. "Sometimes all I can do is eat and eat. But more often I feel so nauseous that even the smell of food makes me gag. I think Ian's death just sent me over the edge, and I don't know, maybe I'm depressed. He was always there to support me... through the other stuff. Now that he's gone, I have no one to encourage me to get up, get dressed, or eat something. I just need a cocktail of things to get me back on track."

She nodded her head the whole time in a way that silently said, I hear you, I understand. Her face was warm and sympathetic.

"I'm sorry you are going through that, but we are going to help as best as we can. I'm going to have the nurse come in and do the basics and then I'll come back to discuss where we go from there." She put her hand on my shoulder and gave it a little squeeze before exiting, leaving me alone in the cold empty room.

They took my height. No change. They took my weight. The number surprised me. I hadn't realized I'd gained any weight. My blood pressure was higher than normal. Then I walked into the bathroom, attempted to pee in the cup and then slid it into the silver cabinet. So, what if I'd gained some weight and my blood pressure was spiking from the anxiety? Considering everything that had happened, I think that was to be expected. At this point, I was just thankful I was getting up and showering occasionally.

Back in the room, I waited for Dr. Katz to return. I stared at the cheap artwork on the wall, three kittens in a basket. Her knock came from the other side of the door and startled me.

"Come in!" I shouted.

When she entered, I couldn't read her expression. She removed the stethoscope from around her neck and placed it on the counter next to her and then leaned against the small countertop.

Just give me the paper for the Xanax, I thought to myself. I'll take two Xanax and have a mug full of merlot. Maybe that will finally bring me a decent night's sleep.

"When was your last period?" she asked, while looking down at the clipboard in her hand.

This question took me by surprise and I tried to remember. "I honestly have no clue. I haven't been keeping track of that or much else lately."

She nodded to show both understanding and sympathy. "Brittany," she said and then took a pause that felt as if it ripped a seam into time. "You're pregnant."

ELEVEN

Everything stopped around me as if I was an actress in a movie and the viewer pressed pause. But my mind did not get the message because it went at warp speed, question after question forming. How can I do this alone? How can I take care of someone else when I can't even take care of myself right now? How cruel is it that Ian's first child will be born after his death, not even knowing what he helped to create? And then like a stab to the heart—How can I bring someone I would cherish into this world when I know what effect I have on everyone I love? I can't have this baby, can I?

I felt the warmth of my hand on my stomach. My hand created a shield around my womb, blocking out this evil and cruel world. A moment that should be filled with joy was overshadowed by dread.

"How far along?" I asked.

"You'll have to see your OB/GYN for that."

"Yeah, okay," I said.

Then a glimpse of my future flashed in my mind. It showed me holding a baby wrapped in a pastel yellow blanket. Their warm, tiny, wrinkled fingers wrapping around my index finger. A sense of calm that I hadn't felt in over five years rushed through me. Despite my apprehension, something locked into place. I could see myself as a mother for the first time. I realized I wanted this baby more than anything.

It would be difficult to do this alone—the most difficult thing I'd ever done, I imagined. It certainly wasn't how I pictured raising my child. This baby is a miracle, like every child, but it will also be a connection to Ian and my only family member. Something within me switched and the dread melted away and was replaced by a resolve to do whatever needed to keep my child safe.

I allowed a smile to touch the edge of my lips and it grew from there until I was beaming at the doctor. "Thank you," I said.

She took a step towards me. "Make that appointment as soon as possible. In the mean time, I'll print out a list of all the things to do and to avoid during pregnancy."

After thanking her again, she stood up and left. Alone in the room, I allowed the tears to fall.

There was only one place I could think to go with this news. One place I could let this information out into the world.

I placed my hand over the cold gray stone. Crouching down, I ran my fingers over his name: Ian Foster, 1984-2024. Seeing the years of his birth and death far too close together broke something inside of me. I know people will walk through this cemetery and this headstone will catch their eye. They'll think 'Only forty? That's a shame. Wonder what happened.' And then they will go about their day and never give it a second thought. He deserved so much more. For me, he was more than a passing thought. He was my every thought.

"I have something I need to tell you," I said quietly to him. "I wish I could have told you in person because I know you would've had the best reaction. But, I'm..." and my voice cracked.

Tears pooled in the corners of my eyes. I took a moment to regain my composure, determined to convey this message with joy, without tears. To say it as if he was still here with me. I inhaled a long and deep breath to prepare to speak again.

"Brittany?" I heard a voice deep and low from above me. I jumped, for an instant thinking Ian had responded to me.

I turned toward the voice and standing behind me, looming over me was a man. It took me a second to recognize him, the context of seeing him here was all wrong. Normally, I only saw Charles in one of Ian's coffee shops.

Charles had been with Ian since day one of his business venture. In fact, he was the first person Ian pitched the idea to. Though he didn't play much of an active role in the business, Charles had invested a substantial amount into the coffee chain. Ian wouldn't have been able to start his dream without his backing.

Though Ian always felt indebted to him, understandably, Charles always rubbed me the wrong way. He always acted like he thought a bit too highly of himself. His black hair was slicked back and he was dressed sharply.

"Charles. I wasn't expecting you to be here," I said as I tried to stand and he extended a hand to help me up.

"I wasn't able to make it to the funeral. I was in Ecuador trying to meet with some coffee farmers. It had been planned a long time ago, by Ian in fact, so unfortunately, I couldn't reschedule." He was saying too much. "Anyway, I thought I'd come pay my respects. I'm so sorry for your loss. Should I leave you?" He looked uncomfortable and he tried to shove his hands into his pockets but his jeans were too tight. Awkwardly, he then interlocked his arms behind his back. He was making me feel nervous for him.

"That was nice of you. I'm sure Ian would have appreciated it." I silently cursed myself for saying the empty cliches that riled me up at his funeral.

He shrugged a little. "How are you holding up?"

"I'm not sure how to answer that. A mess. But still alive. I'm not sure what this level of grief is supposed to look like or how it will evolve from here."

He nodded but was silent for a while, and I liked the silence. It was like a prayer for Ian. We loved you and are holding space for you where you should be, here making a joke at two awkward people trying to navigate an awkward situation. I thought of how he'd probably interject something that would make us all laugh and before I realized it, I was smiling.

Charles looked at me quizzically. "You okay?" He was probably worried I was cracking up right before his eyes.

"As okay as I can be. I think I'm going to head out."

"I'll walk with you, if that's okay?"

I paused, thinking if I should make an excuse so I could walk alone. Nothing came to mind, so I quietly said, "Sure."

There was more silence as we walked along the path. Spring had brought out yellow daffodils and purple lilacs, but it didn't make the place any less depressing. We passed other graves. An entire life diminished to a block of marble. Some simple, some wildly elaborate, like they should be in an art museum. We passed a tombstone of a baby, the date of birth and death the same day and tears began to roll down my cheeks. Charles noticed and put his hand on my back as we continued to walk.

When we got to my car, I tried to block his view of the inside, which was filled with fast food wrappers. It looked more like a large trash can than the passenger side of a car.

"This probably isn't the place, but can I ask you something?" he asked as he rubbed his forehead.

"Sure," I responded, unsure of where this conversation was going.

"I heard that you didn't think it was a heart attack. That maybe something else was going on."

I didn't say anything in response so he continued.

"Do you think Ian's death had anything to do with the business?"

"With Gritty Grinds? I hadn't thought of it, not for a second.

Why would you think that?" It was one of the most successful local coffee shops and they helped the community by hosting several fundraisers throughout the years.

I watched as his eyes started looking into my car and shifted a little. I knew there were a few empty cups from his competitor laying in there. Despite the fact that I could have got a free coffee at any of his locations, I didn't know if I could ever set foot in there again.

"The business was expanding and I think some of the smaller coffee shops might have had an issue with the locations we picked. Like the strategy was to pick locations close by, drive down their business and shut them down. Maybe we pissed off the wrong people."

I shook my head. "Ian wasn't killed over a cup of Joe." I thought what happened to him was bigger than this. I didn't say aloud what I was thinking, that his theory wouldn't explain all the other deaths.

"Maybe not. But deciding on what strategy to take was causing a rift between him and Mike."

"How so?"

"Mike wanted to grow the business—and fast! But Ian really wanted to do more research, make sure we weren't hurting any other local shops. He was more cautious."

"More thoughtful," I added. I looked back towards my car and he picked up that I was itching to go.

"You're probably busy, I know and I hate to bring this up, here and now. But we'll have to meet up soon to discuss what happens with the business."

I knew he still had a ton of money tied up in it and he wanted to make sure he got his money back. "Yeah, yeah. Of course. I don't have any of the documents though." A look of confusion flashed over his face. "You'll have to talk to Mike so he can get this all sorted. I probably need to call him too, actually." I had a few questions about how the assets would be divided.

He nodded. "Okay, I'll let you go. Be well, Brittany." I watched him leave before deciding what to do next.

I went to the cemetery with one goal, and now the moment had been ruined. There was just too much on my mind to deliver this special news. I would have to come back another time.

I got in my car and glared out the window as I thought about what he said. I doubted his theory was correct, but I did know someone willing to look into it.

TWELVE

E ntering my home, with this new life inside of me, I looked around at the decor. A monochromatic white theme and expensive fabrics throughout screamed that we were nowhere near thinking about kids. We had talked about how we would probably want to have children one day but hold it off as long as we thought possible. Though I was in my mid-thirties, my biological clock wasn't ticking loudly yet.

There was a lot we'd wanted to do before settling down with kids. We'd wanted to travel more. My goal was for Japan and his was Australia. We'd wanted to build up our savings so we were prepared for the ever-increasing expenses of raising a child. Money for college, weddings and all the other big-ticket things that came with having kids. I still liked to stay up late, sleep in and just have time to myself. Yes, we wanted a little family, but that was probably a good two or three years out for us.

I ran my hands over the white couch. The small pops of color we had in the room caught my attention—an expensive piece of artwork hanging on the wall, a red vase on the mantelpiece. These had been items we purchased to reward ourselves for various work-related achievements. My life had drastically changed and now my view on these items and this room had also changed. It had been a declaration of our rejection of social expectations but now it was just a large obstacle. It was going to take a hell of a lot of work to get this place ready for a child. I needed to baby proof the house, set up a nursery, sell off some of the white furniture that wouldn't remain that color long with a little one in the house.

In addition to preparing for the new arrival, I needed to figure out this black cloud that has been following me for the last five years. Who had been targeting me? I took out my tan leather journal and made a list of avenues to look down.

Connection to Ian's coffee business?
Kelly?
My job?

My gut told me that my first mission was to figure out who Kelly was. I opened up Facebook, entered Ian's email, and then the password, which consisted of my name and our anniversary. A small but sweet gesture. Unlike his phone, apparently, he didn't change this one.

I was logged in and scrolling through his friends list, which was quadruple the size of mine. Friends from different points in his life, coworkers, people from his bowling league. Ian was such an easy-going and kind person that he easily made friends everywhere he went.

I didn't see a Kelly, though I know people use fake names on social media sometimes to avoid employers finding them. I switched to looking closely at each face. Finally, I found her, but she didn't look like she was some elementary school friend. The single photo of her, at the coffee shop for a holiday party, was from two years back. She was wearing a tight red dress and her arm was wrapped around Louis, a longtime barista at his

Chestnut Street location. So, I assumed she was either Louis' wife or girlfriend. I leaned back in my swivel chair, thinking about why this lady would lie to me about how she knew Ian.

While I was deep in thought, Rosco scratched at the door, signaling he wanted to go out, and it made me smile how human like the action was, like he was knocking on the door. I had taken to talking to him like he's a human, since he was often my only chance at interaction.

"Okay, okay. Just let me change into my sweats." As he didn't understand, he continued to scratch.

Once dressed, I leashed him up and tossed on my coat. The sight of bright white stars glittering across the sky surprised me as I hadn't realized how late it was. The day got away from me. "Just a quick one," I told him as if he had a concept of time.

Being out at night made me nervous. Being alone made me nervous. Just living made me nervous. Rosco was a great dog, but I don't think he'd do much to protect me. His sweet nature meant he wouldn't hurt a fly.

Kelly said she lived two streets over by the elementary school. I decided to walk that way, just to see if I saw any evidence of her actually living there, maybe spot her in the window. It was probably a long shot but this desire to know was like an itch I couldn't scratch.

Rosco bobbed along with me, unconcerned that I was doing my own attempt at PI work and the dangers that might bring upon us. We walked along the street and no one was around. Not Kelly. Not anyone. It gave me an eerie feeling, so I picked up my pace and tried to get home as soon as possible.

I couldn't escape the unsettling feeling and once we got to the house, I quickly double locked the door behind us. Rosco pulled on his leash, which he never did inside. "You okay, boy?" I asked, as I undid the clip and he ran off. I'm not usually so paranoid but I went around and checked that all the windows were shut and locked too. The doorbell camera had a good view of my entire tiny yard and I watched the live footage for a while, making sure there was no one lurking nearby. As the sky darkened, it became hard to make out the image and a few times I froze thinking someone was in my parking spot, but then it just turned out to be a neighbor walking by.

My eyelids became heavy to the point I was fighting with them to stay open. I gave in and climbed into bed, even though it was still pretty early in the evening. My sleep schedule, if you can call it that, was all over the place.

Rosco jumped into my bed, his large and heavy body creating a thud as he landed. He'd never slept here before Ian passed away. When Ian lived here, he had a big blue bed set up for him in the living room. The first night without the security of my husband by my side, I patted the bed, eager for some comfort and he hasn't left since.

I nuzzled my head into his and said, "You are going to be a big brother."

He licked my face in approval, and the warmth of his body felt like a hug. The first one I decided to share this major life milestone with was a dog. Because who else did I have to tell? I laid there like that for a while, my tears wetting his soft golden fur.

Thirteen

Three-hundred and thirty days. My phone was aglow with that reminder. Every day it told me how many days until the next March 13.

After Ian died, I had no one left and thought I should turn off this notification. But I didn't because it had moored me to the emotional ebb and flow of my year. End of March, washed in sadness. April bringing a relief that everyone would be safe for the next eleven months. February flooded with an overwhelming anxiety that consumed me.

There was no one left for them to take until I got the news... or was I next?

This countdown was now a ticking time bomb, reminding me how long I had until they struck again. It's how many days I had to find out what was happening and how to correct it. As the thought passed, I ridiculed myself for how ludicrous that sounded, as if I was some crime solving superhero.

Unlocking this mystery could open up more wounds than it may heal. It may uncover secrets I wasn't ready to know. I dialed my former work-place and asked to be put through to my boss.

"We need to meet," I said hurriedly, skipping all greetings.

"Brittany, that isn't a good idea."

"I need to."

"I just can't," he said, sounding annoyed.

"Yes, you can. You owe it to me after firing me for something completely out of my control. An action I'm not sure was quite legal. And when did you do this? During the greatest tragedy of my life. You took the last thing I had going for me."

He let out a sigh. "Damn it! Brittany, why do you have to make me say this? No one wants to be around you, okay? Don't you get that? They are scared."

Silence cut deep as I tried to process what he just said. I cleared my throat. "Okay," I said slowly, giving myself some time to think about how to respond. His declaration took all the wind out of my sails and I spoke with less confidence than before. "Well, can we at least talk now?"

"Fine. What do you need?" His voice was so dripping with impatience that I could almost feel his agitation through the receiver.

"I need to know if there was anything I was involved in, unknowingly, that could have given someone a grudge against me."

A low, mocking laugh came through the line and I flashed red hot with anger as I gripped the phone tighter and tighter.

I managed to keep the rage out of my voice. "Can you please answer the question?"

"You're asking me to tell you to expose some criminal activity that's never been exposed before? It's an insane question. Everything we do here is on the up and up. Alright? I want you to get the answers you are seeking but you're going to seriously need to work on your interviewing skills if you plan to make any progress in trying to find a solution." I was too stunned to say anything so he continued. "We're all sorry about what's happened to you. Really, we are. I know you won't believe it but everyone here feels terrible. But I can assure you what's happened has ZERO links to our office, our company, our clients or our employees. I wish you the best of luck, Brittany."

"Okay, well..." and then I saw he had hung up.

Bastard. I slammed the phone down hard on the marble counter. My crime solving, superhero bravado seemed even more silly now and I was furious at myself, at these circumstances, at everyone and everything.

I took out my portfolio of ads that I had created. I flipped through each one, examining it and then researched the company. I did this page after page, for hours. The research yielded no results and I thought about what he said. 'You're going to seriously need to work on your interviewing skills if you plan to make any progress in trying to find a solution.'

I was completely out of my league, emotionally defeated, and I didn't know where to go from here.

Fourteen

I went to the OB/GYN and found out I was eleven weeks along. The app on my phone said the baby was the size of a fig. I held out my hand, imagining a fig there. Small but strong. I still had so long to go, so many weeks to be consumed with worry.

There was so little I had control over in my life. The one thing I could do was take the absolute best care of my body for my baby. Learning about pregnancy and healthy habits became my religion and my body was its shrine. I spent my days reading and implementing what I learned. The vitamins, walks, prenatal yoga, new healthy (though not enjoyable) diet.

Research also recommended reducing stress and that seemed to be the one area I couldn't seem to help. Each day I was terrified that I'd lose the baby naturally or unnaturally. When I felt the stress stirring inside of me, I gently wrapped my arms around my small baby bump, trying to create a barrier between the life inside of me and the outside world.

I'd been lurking in pregnancy online forums since I got the news from Dr. Katz, never commenting, just reading. I saw the anxieties women felt. Will my pregnancy go well? Will the baby be healthy? Will I be a good mom? How long before I can sleep like a normal human again? The worries were overwhelming to begin with. The added stress in my life had to be pushing me to abnormally unhealthy levels. There were moments when I couldn't help but spiral with thoughts of everything that could go wrong.

I peered out the window and noticed that the sky was deepening its shade of blue each passing minute. Before it hit navy blue, I needed to take Rosco out. I grabbed his leash with the Phillies logo all up and down it, and my heart ached for Ian. God, he loved his sports teams so much. Baseball was his favorite and so much so he even had to adorn the dog with its logo. And of course, there was the coffee shop, a little tribute to his favorite mascot. Good memories of different sporting events came back to me, as I asked him question after question trying to understand the game. He'd always laugh good-naturedly and then explain it, though I'd never really understood so we would repeat the ritual at the next game. Regardless, those were the best times together.

Rosco jumped up from the couch when he noticed I had the red, white and blue leash, his tail wagging wildly. I put on my headphones and clipped the leash to his harness. Did he even miss Ian anymore? What I wouldn't give to swap places with this creature who got so excited to go out to pee and then slept the rest of the day.

I walked quickly, my sneakers making an audible sound with each hastened step. If I could walk fast enough, I could count this as a bit of exercise for the week. I was fiddling with my phone, trying to find a song that wouldn't remind me of Ian when I heard my name.

"Brittany!" I looked up to see her.

"Oh...hi," I stammered, trying to pull out my earbuds while still having control over Rosco's leash, no easy task since he was excited to see this stranger. He pulled hard on the leash, trying to jump on Kelly. My hands clenched around the leash as I braced my feet so he didn't knock us both over.

"Sorry, he doesn't get out much now, and he's just excited to see another living being."

She smiled down at the golden dog and then looked at me, her face transformed with concern. "How are you holding up?"

"Fine."

"I was thinking it'd be good if we got together to talk sometime. Would you like to meet up for coffee?"

Not at all, not with her, not with anyone at this point. But part of me was curious too. And I had wished for someone to talk to about Ian, hadn't I? "Sure," I said with a slight shrug.

"When is a good time?"

I cracked a weak smile. "Literally anytime." The last time I had to be anywhere was my husband's funeral and then some doctor's appointments. Not exactly a busy social life. I had all the time in the world.

Unlike the last time we ran into each other, we actually set plans and exchanged phone numbers. We decided to meet up early tomorrow and I wasn't sure how I felt about the whole thing.

I walked into the diner and the smells and chatter overwhelmed my senses. Instinctively, I put my hand over my mouth, worried I might get sick. Then the nausea passed and I stepped further into the place. I saw her sitting in the tan leather booth, her long red nails moving across the small menu that listed several sugary lattes. For a moment, I thought to run, to back out and text that something came up. But then she saw me and waved.

I weaved around waiters and diners to get to where she sat. "Hi," I greeted and she smiled. But I noticed something in her eyes. Her expression said she was surprised I actually showed up. I was too.

As soon as I sat down, I looked over the menu. A minute later the waitress took our order. It gave me a second to settle into the situation.

After our coffees were put on the table, she grabbed the sugar container and dumped an ungodly amount into her cup. "You've been through a lot," she said, still dumping in sugar. My eyebrows furrowed, why do people keep telling me this as if I didn't know. It was as if they felt the need to announce, *Hello! Grief is in the room with us.*

"I suppose you have too."

"It doesn't comp—," and she stopped herself.

"You said, you knew my husband from school?" She made a sound in agreement as she took a sip of her drink. "Which school?"

"Hmmm...???"

"I said, which school?" I enunciated each word, trying to keep the edge out of my voice. Her eyes widened like a deer in head-lights. Something wasn't right. "What the hell is going on here?" I demanded.

She laughed a little and raised both hands. "You caught me!"

Caught her? What did she even mean by that? "Were you sleeping with Ian?" I practically yelled and other diners turned to look at me, eager to see the drama, others blushed and looked away.

"No! God, no. Definitely not."

"I don't believe you," I said lowering my tone of voice, trying to get the onlookers to go back to their meal.

"I'm married."

"And? It's not like that has stopped people before. Tell me who you are right now and why you've come after me because I'm about seven seconds away from pouring this blueberry syrup on your head," I said as I grabbed the glass bottle from the edge of the table.

She used her hands to signal for me to calm down. I hate when people do that, and it only made me angrier.

"Okay, put the syrup down. I'll tell you, but I need you to hear me out. The whole thing before you react."

I did as I was told despite the adrenaline pumping through my veins. I put down the glass and it made a loud clank as it hit the faux marble table.

"I'm a local journalist. My husband, well now he's about to be my ex-husband, worked for Ian so he had told me your story awhile back. And I thought it would be—"

"You mothe—" I kept my voice low but it was still filled with rage.

"Hear me out!" she said as she waved her hands in a downward motion. I didn't say anything so she continued. "I've been working at a small local paper for years now and I've been trying to pitch this idea to them, to cover your story. I've been researching it on my own for over a year now. So back when things were good, my husband introduced me to Ian and he did sit down with me for an interview. It was right after your sister died. We met once, at one of his shops. We had a coffee and talked. That's it."

"He never told me about that. Did he even know you were a journalist?"

"Not exactly. My husband just told him I was interested in maybe helping in some capacity. He didn't seem to ask too many questions."

"That's not an interview! You bit—" I stopped myself, teetering between anger and not wanting to cause a scene. She took Ian's trusting nature and used it against us. There was no way he would have talked to someone about Melissa's death if he knew it was going to be used for profit or even to bring more attention to us.

Our waitress returned with our meals, putting an egg white veggie omelet in front of her and a stack of blueberry pancakes in front of me, which I quickly covered in syrup.

"Can you please try to see this from another angle? This could benefit you, too. I know I went about it all wrong. And I'm sorry for that. I should have been upfront with you. I was hoping to get to know you informally first, but obviously that didn't work out. But I can help you."

"How? There's nothing left," I said as tears rimmed my eyes and then flowed. I grabbed a napkin from the dispenser at the head of the table and ran it along my cheeks.

"I want to start a podcast about you. But I'll only do it if you agree to it and want to participate...to whatever extent you are comfortable."

Without even realizing it, I was shaking my head no. Being a journalist, she was undeterred so she kept pitching the idea.

"Think of how this can benefit you! If the podcast takes off, more people will hear your story. That means more tips coming in, and more for the police to work with. Often if these things go viral, it can get the police to be more involved and allocate more resources towards the case. Maybe we can even help you raise reward money. Maybe even figure this thing out. Solve it!" She spoke faster with each sentence. Her voice was on the edge of excitement and I pulled back, uncomfortably.

I rolled my eyes. "Podcasts don't solve murders. You're thinking a bit too highly of yourself."

Kelly shrugged. "Maybe I am. But what do you have to lose?"

Her words stung, but I realized she had a point. Plus, all those things she mentioned could really help me get some answers. "I suppose nothing at this point."

"You don't need to say anything now, but will you consider it? Think about it awhile and get back to me."

"Yeah, I'll spend some time thinking about it. But stop running into me and my dog. I'll contact you if I decide this is a good idea. And don't hold your breath. Right now, I'm leaning towards, hell no."

"Well, at least you are honest." She took a bite of her omelet, but I had no appetite.

"Yeah, unlike you," I said deadpan.

She did a little shimmy like she was shaking off my insult.

"That's fair. But if you decide you want to explore what the podcast would look like or just ask any questions, here is my card with my business email."

The card landed in front of me and coordinated with her manicured nails. This lady was unbelievable. I tossed the card into my tote bag without care.

Though there were several clear possible benefits, there could also be some very alarming consequences. Like what if public opinion swayed the police to look at me as a suspect? Or if it gave the murderer incentive to find me, to come after me next?

FIFTEEN

My house had become a graveyard of Ian's things. Each item around the house was like a shard of glass that I stepped on with bare feet. It tore my flesh wide open, stinging, bleeding out. His pile of dirty laundry, sitting there nearly two months, still in the corner, his toothbrush, the last book he was reading on the nightstand, the ending never to be finished. These everyday items were testaments that he was here with me. I couldn't throw them away; not even put them away. Putting his things away felt like I was putting our life away, wiping out his existence. Shoving it out of my mind and memory. However, keeping his things around felt like I was taunting myself with his absence.

I couldn't win.

I wished he was here to tell me what to do about this podcast idea. He'd probably encourage me to do it so I could get some answers or at least feel proactive. Though I couldn't be positive if that's correct or not, I was pretty sure that's the case. I envisioned him sitting next to me on the couch, and I am telling him all about it with a mug of red wine in my hand. He'd nod and consider all the pros and cons thoughtfully, and then he'd say, "Might as well, right?"

It made me feel a little better that I was even considering it.

I dug around in my large tote bag, shifting through old receipts, pens, unopened mail, and other knick-knacks until I found it. With Kelly's business card in my hand, I twirled it between my fingers, watching it flip back and forth. After my failed attempt at detective work, I felt a little embarrassed about what I was about to do. I grabbed my laptop and put her name into the search bar. I needed to see her work for a few reasons.

First, I needed to verify that she actually worked where she said she did. Second, I wanted to see if her work was any good. If it was, it would give me more confidence that this podcast could be done well. If the podcast wasn't good quality, if it didn't go viral or at least become semi-popular, this could all backfire on me or just be a huge waste of time. I had a lot of time on my hands, but I didn't want to spend it exposing my trauma to a stranger if it didn't have the results I was seeking.

All the top hits were links to her articles in the local newspaper. There was a 'hard-hitting' article about the increased traffic in the area. I clicked the link and it brought me to the website for the Collingswood Chronicle.

Flashing at the top of the screen was a big red banner announcing it was closing after one-hundred and twenty-five years in business. I'd never had a newspaper delivered to my house since I became an adult but I remember my friend Amanda's brother, who was several years older than we were, was a paper boy. I recalled after a sleepover, seeing him stacking up the papers into his wagon early in the morning. I felt sadness that this era was coming to an end.

Click and read, click and read. I poured over many of her previous articles. They went back three years, as she stated, and covered a wide range of local topics. It was all legit and her articles were well written. The idea of participating was beginning to seem more plausible.

I toyed around with the idea, trying to envision myself being a part of something that could possibly go viral. There have been true crime podcasts that spread like wildfire and changed the whole narrative, even bringing about a retrial. What if something like that happened here? I needed answers, and right now, this might be my only hope. The more I played with the idea, the more I thought I might do it.

I propped her business card on the laptop screen and then opened an email to type in the message.

I'M NOT READY TO TALK ON THE RECORD ABOUT WHAT HAPPENED. BUT I GIVE YOU MY PERMISSION TO START THE PODCAST.

GOOD LUCK.

My finger hovered over the trackpad for a few seconds, questioning if this was the right choice. I took a deep breath, pressed send, and prayed this wasn't the wrong decision.

Opening another tab, I watched two episodes of some home décor show. Her response came back as I was about to start the third.

GREAT!

I'M LOOKING FORWARD TO TELLING YOUR STORY.

I rolled my eyes, closed the email tab, and went back to watching the third episode while stewing about her response. Nothing about this situation should cause someone to be 'looking forward' to it. This was part of my hesitation. I'd listened to enough true crime podcasts to know that people's grief became their paycheck. So, they sensationalize, they will have banter with their co-hosts, all while discussing horrific events. I tried to listen to a few different shows a while back that a coworker had recommended, but they honestly made me sick to my stomach, especially the ones where kids were hurt.

It wasn't just the style of these shows that bothered me. I knew Kelly would profit from this. I knew she was using my grief as her career stepping stone. She's selling trauma porn. So, while I didn't approve, I also knew that I needed answers before all of this ate me alive—or something else happened.

And now, as the subject and possible participant in a podcast, I had to wonder if I was serving myself on a platter to whoever was causing this.

Sixteen

My phone illuminated in the pitch-black room. My eyes took a moment to adjust to the bright screen that read 2:46am and then I saw the text, from an unknown number.

> You shouldn't have done that.

I sucked in a breath and felt my muscles tense. Was this about the podcast? But I hadn't told anyone. There wasn't anyone to tell. If not that, what were they talking about?

Rosco lifted his head and then plopped it back on the bed. I typed back,

> Wrong number.

And immediately saw they were typing a response. I prayed it said an apology so I could relax and attempt to go back to bed.

> No, this is the right number. And you shouldn't have done that, Brittany.

I jolted up in bed. The phone in my hand was vibrating and I realized it was from my hands trembling so badly. I started mumbling aloud, a habit I had picked up in my loneliness.

"Who do I call? What do I do? What can I do?" My voice was weak and pathetic.

I dialed Kelly.

"Brittany?" Her confused voice came through the line.

"Did you tell anyone about the podcast?"

"It's three am," Kelly responded, clearly still half asleep.

"Did you?!"

"Yeah, of course. I bounced the idea off people before I approached you. And..."

"What?!" I got out of bed and began to pace around the room. Rosco sat up and watched me move around for a moment but then settled his head back down. He was softly snoring moments later. So much for man's best friend.

"I've tried to connect with some sponsors. But the funds would go towards hiring a PI, this guy Hank I've been talking to, and setting up a tip line," she said defensively. "Also, I accidentally posted about it, I was trying to schedule the post on Instagram and, apparently, set it for the wrong date. When I realized, I deleted it right away."

I sat on the bed and pet Rosco's soft head, more for my benefit than his. Her carelessness floored me. I had never despised and needed someone so much. I reread the text messages and knew I needed to be with someone, anyone right now. I couldn't be alone. Not when it felt like someone was coming after me.

"Can you come over?"

"Now?!"

"Yeah. Use it for your fucking podcast. 'She called me at three am in a panic.'" I told her my address and she blew out a breath into the phone. "I'll be there in fifteen to twenty minutes."

There was a knock at the door and Rosco responded by running to the door and barking loudly. He did not appreciate middle of the night visitors. I dashed over and shushed him. "Who is it?" I asked through the door.

"Who else would be here at three am?" Her voice was a combination of annoyance and fatigue.

I opened the door just a crack and immediately saw her bright blonde hair. When she walked in, I took note that she had bothered to put on mascara and lip gloss.

"I don't like you," I told her flatly.

She huffed out a laugh. "So why am I here?" She walked past me in her matching pajamas, top and bottom covered with little pink roses. Kelly tossed her purse on the couch before sitting down. She rapidly blinked her eyes as she yawned.

"Because I need you. I think." I shoved my phone into her hand and then sat next to her. "I just got this, right before I called you."

She raised her eyebrows as she looked at the message. "It's ominous. But could easily be a prank. Your case is being talked about all over social media right now."

"What do you mean, all over social media? I thought you were going to be the only one covering it."

"I don't really have any control over who talks about it. I'm hoping we are the first in-depth true crime podcast, but yeah, there are videos all over TikTok. You haven't seen them?"

I shook my head, horrified that all this was happening without my knowledge. "I don't even have a TikTok account."

She pulled out her phone and tapped it a few times, her long nails clicking the screen before turning it to me.

"Crime with Christal was the biggest one to cover it."

I stared at the screen. She posted it yesterday and it had nearly a quarter of a million views. My jaw dropped open. Kelly leaned over and playfully guided my jaw closed with her hand.

"Everyone has their theories, as you can see by the comments section. And some people get too invested in it and like to interject themselves into the story by creating their own response videos and so it spreads out from there."

"It isn't a story. It is my life." I felt my pulse quicken.

"I know. So, let's start with that. First podcast you can introduce yourself. Let people know that you aren't some story to sensationalize. Let them see you as a real person, a person who is deeply grieving and struggling. Bring them into the mix to try to help us solve what's happening here."

I nodded. "I'm still not sure if this is the right thing to do, but I have to do something at this point. I owe it to everyone." I supposed if this was already being talked about, it was better if I had some control of the narrative. "Let's do it."

"Great," she said, unable to control her excitement. Kelly reached into her purse and pulled out a small notebook and pen. We discussed plans for the first episode as she wrote down our ideas. Understandably, we were both sleep deprived, so the notes we took were barely legible and the ideas were half-baked.

The next thing I knew, Rosco pawed at my side. This was his routine for requesting to go out in the morning. That's when I realized I had fallen asleep beside her on the couch.

"Kelly," I said as I tapped her shoulder. "It's the morning."

She blinked her eyes several times, the notebook still in her lap, and then sat up rubbing her neck. "Morning," she said as she stretched her arms above her.

I walked to get Rosco's leash and he followed me, his claws making a constant click clack sound as he jaunted across the marble tile.

"I'm going to see myself out. Should we meet up today? Maybe around three to finish planning?" She looked at her notebook and furrowed her brow. "Or maybe start planning?" She laughed. "Did one of us really suggest getting a therapy goat for recording sessions?"

"We were tired!" I said, defending our bizarre, yet adorable, idea.

I agreed to meet up, as my stomach clenched. Somehow, overnight I had become more involved than I wanted to be in this already.

She made her way to the door as I stood there with Rosco now on his leash. Seeing her open the door caused him to try to pull forward but I remained in place. "Hey, Kelly," I said and she turned toward me, raising her eyebrows. "We'll only talk about those five years. I won't discuss anything else. Everything from before that time period is completely off the table."

She scanned my face. "Yeah, sure. Absolutely," she said and then she walked out the door. I prayed she could keep her promises.

SEVENTEEN

Later that day, Kelly was sitting across from me on the white couch. Her legs were folded criss-cross like a child would do in school. Though we weren't recording, I knew this conversation would be uncomfortable. I shifted in my seat and then crossed my legs, not fully ready for this conversation. She wanted to hear me go through each 'incident' as she called them.

"I want to hear your side of it before we start recording," she said and I knew the reality of it was she needed to see if I was ready for all this. "Let's start at the beginning," she said in a way that seemed too authoritative for someone perched on my couch like a kindergartner. "The first person to pass was your best friend. Katie in March of 2020. Can you tell me a little about her?"

Just hearing her name, I couldn't help but smile, recalling her kindness and our deep connection. Kelly nodded along as I recounted story after story, trying to paint a picture of how incredible a person she was and all that she meant to me. I wasn't sure words could really capture a strong friendship like ours had been. It was something that needed to be felt.

"Tell me about what happened to Katie on the night she died."

"She didn't die. She was murdered," I said, a lump the size of a golf ball forming in my throat. I recounted all the horrific details, as much as I could remember. Your mind tends to block out some of the trauma just to cope and I hoped she didn't mistake my omissions as being cagey.

"What do you think happened to her?"

"The police said it was a random attack. They never found her killer."

She leaned forward towards me. "What do you think happened to her?" she repeated with a strong emphasis on you.

"I think someone knew how much she meant to me and took her."

"Who could that be?"

I'd thought about this for years of course but I could never find any possibility that made sense. "I think that's what we're all trying to figure out."

"What was that first year like for you?"

"It was incredibly difficult. I spoke to Katie nearly every day. We spent time together most weekends. Her absence could be felt in my daily routine. But I had no idea that this was just the beginning. That in fact, her death was part of my new routine as sick and horrible as that sounds. I think about that first year and wish I could have warned myself of what was to come." I looked down at my hands before saying, "I don't really know what else to say about it."

"Let's talk about your parents."

I sucked in a breath, surprised with how quickly we were jumping to the next tragedy. "Okay," I said.

"How was your relationship with them?"

I knew this question would come and had practiced what I would say and how I would say it. "It was wonderful. I couldn't have asked for better parents. Melissa and I had a good childhood," I lied. The truth was too complicated to explain to a stranger, and that complexity would be too easy to misjudge as callousness.

"The police report found no evidence of foul play. It seemed like reckless driving."

"By a hit-and-run driver. Who was never found. That's suspicious to me. Don't you think?"

She shrugged. "Normally, I'd say no. But given the circumstances, I see how it could be."

"And there's another issue. There were mechanical problems with the car, which they chalked up to normal malfunction. They didn't deem foul play, but it seems there could have been something tampered with. And what about the fact that neither of them had even a speeding ticket in the last decade? And now they're on the road acting like road racers?" I had been gesturing wildly as I spoke and then became self-conscious. I slipped my hands under my lap to stop my erratic movements.

"So, you don't think it was an accident?"

"Not a chance. For a while, I just believed what was told to me, but after this happened again the next year, I couldn't ignore it. Everything had to be connected—the same date, with me at the center. There were no coincidences in all this." I crossed my arms.

"I know this is hard but you are doing a great job. If it is okay, let's talk about the next year then. The following year there was Amanda. She's the one that really baffles me."

Kelly looked off into the distance, like she was thinking of what to say next and I felt my anxiety rise with each second of silence. My heart started to pound wildly and I could see it beating through my shirt. The Amanda piece always baffled me too—like she was connected but she wasn't.

"How long had it been since you had spoken to her?"

I pretended to be thinking about this by rubbing my chin. Then I thought it looked too dramatic and quickly withdrew my hand from my face. "Hmmm, must have been around third or forth grade."

"What happened?"

"Well, I moved away. And it was before the internet so there wasn't an easy way to keep in touch, especially being so young. I suppose we could have been pen-pals or something but that just didn't happen."

"Would you say the grieving process was easier with Amanda?"

I pulled back, the question catching me off guard. "Well, every life is precious, so I don't want to put it like that. The death of my best friend and my parents hit me harder, obviously, since I saw them more often than Amanda. But it was incredibly sad. She was talented and so loved by her siblings and parents. They were very protective of her. I do recall that." I tensed up, wishing I hadn't said that. I shouldn't have brought them into the conversation and made a mental note not to mention that when we did record. "My sister was actually friends with her sister," I added.

"Then you suffered another big loss when your sister passed away. What are your thoughts there?" I looked beyond her, unable to meet her gaze at that moment.

This whole conversation was too matter-of-fact, moving from death to death so quickly. I held up my palm, just needing a minute. I took my pointer fingers and dragged them across the bottom of my eyes, trying to absorb the tears each time they threatened to fall.

"They said she overdosed," I whispered as I leaned over to grab a tissue off the end table.

She looked down at her notes. "I couldn't find any information on what the autopsy found. What did she overdose on?"

"They said sleeping pills and anti-anxiety pills."

"So, you don't agree?"

"No," I said flatly.

"I think it could make sense though. She overdosed, intentionally or accidentally, on the anniversary of your parents' death. Maybe it was too much to handle, so she turned to those things to cope."

"But it doesn't make any sense, for a few reasons. First, I was with her that day, practically the entire day in fact. There wasn't any hint that she was suffering that badly. Sure, she was sad, but that was to be expected. She didn't seem like she was going to hurt herself. Second, Melissa didn't do anything like that. I'm telling you, I knew my sister!" I was trying not to yell, but the irritation was thick in my voice.

"People have secrets."

"Secrets. Sure. Hiding a prescription drug problem from the person closest to you? That seems harder to buy."

"What if she didn't have a drug problem? What if she tried it for the first time, to try to escape the pain, and didn't know how much to take? Do you think that's possible?"

"No. How would she have gotten the stuff? The fact is that they couldn't find any evidence of her buying pills, knowing anyone who sold them. She had no prescription."

Kelly was nodding her head in agreement. "And then..."

Before the words were off her lips, tears were running down my cheeks as I wiped under my eyes with the tear-soaked tissue. I uncrossed my legs and started to pull myself into a ball, a small comfort. Suddenly, it became a labor to breathe.

She gave me time to calm down before asking, "Are you ready to talk about it? About—"

"Ian." His name was bittersweet on my lips. I loved saying his name aloud because it was a declaration that he mattered, that our time together, no matter how short, mattered. When you say the name aloud of someone you loved, for that second in time, they still exist. "There's never an easy time to talk about this but I know one thing. This wasn't natural."

"You do know that if something was done to him, that you'd be the most likely suspect."

"Sure. Of course." I began to rub my forehead as I looked down at the ground.

"And that since you're the connection to all these people, there are some people who think you were responsible."

"Yeah, according to social media. All this is pretty shocking to me though. If there was any truth to it, the police would have locked me up by now, right?" I shook my head. "I guess I don't understand how people could be discussing it without looking at all the facts. But I have to know—Is that what you think too?" I asked, wondering where she was going with this.

She paused too long before responding. "No, no, of course not." And then curled her lips into an unnatural smile.

Eighteen

Three days after that, I walked into her makeshift studio, a room in her home recently converted just for this podcast. The butterflies in my stomach were fluttering on overdrive. In the room was a rectangular table, two swivel chairs and two microphones. There was a laptop, a box of tissues and two water bottles set out.

It was our first recording session. Though I had said I didn't want to talk about anything before Katie passed, she opened it up for me to share anything I felt comfortable discussing, to give the listeners a bit of my background. I was able to babble on for the full hour, painting a picture of the ideal childhood.

For our second recording session, things needed to go deeper.

I came wearing a baggy blue dress with little yellow flowers all over it. Being three months pregnant, I was starting to show ever so slightly, but I couldn't let anyone know. In my mind, as long as I was the only one who knew, I could keep him or her safe.

So far, things were going as well as could be expected. I often broke down crying and we had to pause the session a few times but I was expressing what I felt was important.

"All set?" she asked after my requested break.

I nodded and followed her back into the room. I began to

talk, a story that I had pre-scripted and ran over in my mind for the past few days. Everything I said to her was planned. Well thought out and practiced.

Kelly opened her water bottle and took a swig as I continued to tell her my story.

"So, it was basically the perfect marriage. Ian was..." I said into the microphone.

She put down the bottle with a thud and I jumped at the sudden sound.

I covered the microphone, leaning in. "Should I restart that?"

"Why?"

"Because of the noise?"

"No," she said, her facial expression stony.

"Really? Can you still use it? Won't it sound unprofessional?"

Kelly rubbed her hands over her eyebrows, pinching them towards the middle, creating a deep wrinkle that she was way too young for. It was a tick I had come to notice when she was frustrated.

"What's wrong?" I asked as if I didn't know.

"This podcast is boring as shit," she said waving her hands with each word. "You are dancing around all kinds of things. Leaving things out. It sounds so scripted which will come off as inauthentic. No one can help you when you aren't giving them anymore than they can get with a simple Google search."

I swallowed hard. I knew she was right. This had been my third time discussing this with her and I'd completely held back each time. Not because I didn't want to help, but I was just terrified. I wanted to know who was doing this, but what if it led them to me? What if I was next?

"What happened to you is gripping but you're painting fairy tales for me." I pulled back, surprised that she didn't find what I was saying believable. She was unfazed by my reaction and continued. "It's clear from these recordings that what you are saying is the social media version of the truth. Everything put together in a perfect little package. Hiding the secrets inside." She tossed her hands in the air. "I can't put this out into the world. Not with my name on it. It sounds hollow, inauthentic. It could ruin my career before it even starts."

"This isn't about you," I snapped.

She shrugged. "I still have to put my name on it."

Her disappointment in me took me by surprise and to be honest, it stung a little. I started to plead with her because I was desperate for help. I needed answers and I needed this all to end.

I moved my chair closer to her. "Okay, I can...do better. Just give me some constructive criticism."

"I don't know! Say something of value. Say something that will get people invested in the podcast!"

"I'm pregnant," I blurted out.

We both gasped, in shock of my admission. My hand covered my mouth, as if it would reign in the admission I hadn't wanted to let out. I hadn't planned to say it. It definitely wasn't part of my hours of rehearsed story. There was no taking it back now.

"Is it..." and she let her question hang there for me to fill in the blank.

"Jesus. Yes, the baby is Ian's," I replied defensively, shaking my head at the stupidity of the question.

She got up and came around so I stood too. She hugged me, my small bump creating a bit of space between us. "Congratulations," she said and then pulled away.

"But please don't put that in. Not yet," I begged.

Her face said she was thinking about it, thinking of a way to convince me.

"I'm serious," I said sternly. "I didn't mean to tell you. But no one can know. They will come back if they know." Panic arose in my voice.

Her facial expression completely changed. She held up her hand, pinky extended towards me. I smiled weakly and interlocked my trembling pinky with hers, something I hadn't done since I was in elementary school.

"I swear," she said, and in that moment, I believed her.

Nineteen

The next day, I wanted to grab a coffee on the way to Kelly's. A quick in and out was all I could manage at that time. When I walked in, I caught the eyes of a woman and she didn't look away. I walked past a table where one girl leaned in to whisper to another. I started to feel heat flash through me as my brain went into overdrive. It was pounding the same sentence over and over, *They know who you are! They know who you are and they hate you.*

I might have been on the brink of a panic attack, but I told myself I needed to be able to do everyday things and stop allowing my paranoia to take over my life. In spite of that, I felt my feet rushing out of there and towards the car without even grabbing my order. I sat there for several minutes, ringing my hands together to self-soothe. When the panic subsided, I went back in to grab my coffee off the counter, not making eye contact with anyone. Then I made my way to Kelly's house.

It was a fresh slate for the recording. Being that we were both new at this, it would involve some trial and error. We agreed to some boundaries, non-negotiables and expectations. Last night I took some time to reflect on everything we agreed upon and hopefully, I would be able to do better.

I walked into her recording room, closed the door behind us and sat at the small table in the middle. She sat in her swivel chair and I sat in mine, which I used to fidget when the questions started to make me nervous.

"Are you ready?"

I knew what she meant. Am I ready for the real questions? To dive in deep. To be raw and authentic. Or whatever buzz words she had used. "Yes," I said, unsure if that was the truth or not. "Third times the charm, right?" I said in a lame attempt to lighten the mood. She forced a smile and I was already starting to swing the chair from side to side.

Kelly reached for the record button and I drew in a breath while counting to three, hoping to calm my heart which was doing the jitter bug in my chest.

"You've lost six people in five years, each on the exact same day. Some people think you've caused this. What do you say to them?"

I let the accusation hang there, a little stunned. I knew she was going to start asking more difficult questions but this was such a harsh place to start. "I'd ask them why I'd want to punish myself by leaving myself completely alone. The silence, the loneliness are suffocating. I wouldn't wish this on anyone, I know that's a cliche thing to say but our lives are about love and everyone I love is dead."

My hand cupped around my growing belly. I knew in six months that wouldn't be true any longer and before I was even a mother, my mama bear instincts were kicking in.

Kelly raised her eyes in surprise. "Oh my god. That'd be a great name for the podcast. Sorry...sorry that's insensitive, but what do you think?"

Her eagerness made me uneasy. I tried to let my sigh out slowly so she didn't hear how completely exasperated I was. I was sure the microphone would pick up the sound. When she's editing that part out later, I hoped it would be a reminder to her that this isn't a show, it's my nightmarish life.

"I don't care what you call it. I just want you to help me. Next question." I started gnawing on my inner cheek to get out the negative emotions flowing through me, channeling emotional pain to physical pain.

"Looking back on everyone you've lost, do you see a connection between them?"

"Between everyone? Just me." I hunched my shoulders, trying to make myself smaller, trying to take up less space. As if I was too insignificant to have caused all this terror.

"So, what are your theories? Is it all just a coincidence?"

I thought about how to respond to this. "My husband always thought it was a terrible coincidence. I'd tell him that it was impossible, that the odds of this happening were almost nonexistent. When my parents died, he was sure it was a coincidence. Then when Amanda died, he said it wasn't related because I hadn't spoken to her in years. He was adamant that crazy and unbelievable things do happen from time to time. He looked up statistics about families who were all born on the same day. I know he was just trying to make sense of it all for me but that made me angry. I said it wasn't at all the same thing. Because comparing death and birth seemed so callous."

She was looking at me and slightly bobbing her head, encouraging me to continue.

"So, the short answer is, no I really, really doubt that it is a coincidence."

"So, what is it then?"

Her eyes were digging into me. She wouldn't back down and wanted a response. But I had none. I just sat there, staring back at her. My eyes shifted back and forth between her blue eyes. I tried to find the words but nothing came to mind. She hit the button to stop the recording as her icy glare focused on me. Her disappointment was palpable.

TWENTY

At my twelve week visit, I was brought into a small room and asked to lay on the table. In some ways I still found it hard to picture myself as a mother, a single mother. This visit would hopefully make it all feel real.

The woman applied cold jelly to my stomach and then ran the wand along as a grainy image appeared on the screen. I held my breath, waiting for her to say something positive. Each second that ticked by was like an eternity and I started to tell myself that something must be wrong. I squirmed a bit on the table and she said gently, "Stay still, Mama."

"There they are! Heartbeat sounds great." I heard the dub-dub, dub-dub and the rhythmic sound pacified my worries. My muscles let go of the tension they had been holding. I covered my face, hiding my overwhelming relief from this stranger. "It's okay, Mama," she said sweetly. "It's all going to be okay. Baby looks and sounds great."

I smiled at her as she put the wand down but my smile was a lie. She began to wipe the jelly off my stomach. I was thankful that the baby was doing well, but it made me feel Ian's absence. There was a void in the room, where he should be, eagerly looking at the screen, smiling at the image and then planting a kiss on my forehead.

Would I ever feel true joy again? Or would every moment have this huge black hole where he should be? Would every moment that should create happiness be flanked with sadness at his absence?

I thanked her and quickly left.

You never realize that a simple 'I miss you' text is really a prayer until there is nothing left but the missing part. Not the *I*, nor the *you*. That when you quickly said, I love you, before turning off the light, it was the sweetest love poem that will have ever been written for you. That the quick kiss on the cheek goodbye, that lingered for just a second should have been savored and stretched into eternity. So many small, everyday actions that were taken for granted you now want so desperately that it feels like a need stronger than air, like without them you are suffocating.

With those thoughts hovering over me, I turned on the car and drove home, blasting music to drown out reality. The bass so strong it shook my core. Good, I thought. I needed something to awaken the part of me that died with him.

Entering my home, Rosco's nails could be heard clicking towards me. We sat on the couch as I paged through websites for baby decor. The thought was that if I force a normal action, maybe I'll start to have normal feelings.

It was time to fully embrace this pregnancy, and that started with turning our office space into a nursery. As I paged through the pastel pinks, blues and yellows, I got an idea. I typed in 'baseball themed nursery'. Though he couldn't be with me on this journey, I could still honor him. Our baby could still be connected to him through the things he loved in life. Each item added to my cart brought on more tears until I was ugly crying with a cart full of baby items. With the click of 'complete purchase', I had officially started the transition to mom life.

Twenty-One

Kelly had attended some true crime conference out in Las Vegas two weeks ago and we hadn't scheduled the next session. She texted me at the end of the conference, mentioned it went well and she was going to stay out there another week to drive to the Grand Canyon. Part of me wondered if she really was doing that or if she just decided to drop the whole project and wasn't telling me.

Not seeing her meant I was back to being pretty isolated. Eventually, I needed to resume my normal activities instead of hiding in the house, away from the world. For the past few weeks, my biggest outing was grabbing a quick coffee to go. Last time that didn't go well but I couldn't let one experience alter my whole life.

I decided that instead of placing a mobile delivery order for my groceries like I had been doing since Ian passed, I'd go to the store. Baby steps were better than standing still, I told myself.

First stop: coffee. I still couldn't go to Ian's place. It was better to go somewhere that I wouldn't be noticed. I approached the counter and ordered. It rolled off my tongue without thought. "A medium iced caramel latte and a large," and then I stopped, more like froze solid, like a block of ice.

"A large?" the girl behind the counter asked, eyeing the line forming behind me. I shook my head to pull myself out of the distant thought.

"Actually, just a small iced coffee, decaf please."

"Nothing else?"

I shook my head, my throat thick with grief. She scanned my app for payment and then called the next person to the register. I moved out of the way and could feel that my body felt noticeably heavier.

How long until I remembered to just order one coffee? How long before I realized my 'usual' doesn't exist? That I needed to form a new usual. I walked around the counter to the other side of the coffee shop and collected my drink. Trying to find a seat, one hand stinging from the cold, one hand noticeably empty, I thought in that moment that I was a portrait of a widow— wandering aimlessly through the chaos flanked by coldness and emptiness. There was only one free spot left but sitting at the next table over was a couple holding hands.

I need to get the hell out of here, I thought and made my way to the car where I forced myself to take a few sips of the coffee. The small swigs seemed to get stuck in my throat, and I put the cup into the cup holder. I wasn't in the mood for coffee anymore.

It had been years since I had to plan a week's worth of solo meals. In the theme of taking baby steps, I decided to just get some frozen dinners and hoped this trip went smoother than the coffee shop.

My cart squeaked as I turned around the corner. Apparently, everyone else in town wanted frozen food too because it was insanely crowded. I became hyper-focused on my body and the space it was taking up. Trying to navigate the big cart through so many people made me on edge.

The aisle was chilly from doors opening and I shivered a bit. I dodged people on my way to the right section. There were eyes on me. I could feel it but I told myself I was being paranoid again. As I opened the freezer door, two things hit me. Cold air and hushed tones.

"That's her, right?" I heard in a whispered voice.

I looked over to see two college aged girls talking to each other. They were dressed so similarly, hair done the same, face made up identically with heavy makeup. The two girls were practically replicas of each other.

"Looks like her," replied the other girl as they looked over my way.

When I met their gaze, the pair quickly turned away and pretended to be picking out frozen French fries. This time I was not paranoid. They were actually talking about me.

A week's worth of frozen dinners were tossed into the cart without care nor thought. I needed to get out of there as soon as possible. Maybe they weren't talking about me. But it sure seemed like it. Regardless, I felt panic rising in me. It felt like I was on the edge of a cliff, about to deep dive into unknown waters...and I was unsure if I could swim. *Get out, get out,* my brain said on repeat.

I navigated through the aisle and looked for the first illuminated checkout number. Number seven was the only one on and I made a beeline for it. I stacked the frozen meals on the conveyor belt and waited for the person in front of me to finish up. She seemed to take forever paying, looking around in her purse for exact change. I shifted my weight from one foot to another and wanted to scream, "Just give her another $20 and hurry up!"

While watching them fumble to find the last two pennies needed, I thought about how those girls had recognized me and talked about me like I was some science specimen. My humanity was lost in the sensationalism of the story. The more I thought about it the angrier I became.

I was on edge when the cashier scanned my first meal and said, "How are you today?"

"What's that supposed to mean?" I snapped.

She furrowed her brows and I could tell she wasn't in the

mood to take any nonsense from anyone today. "It's a standard greeting that people say. And normal people respond, 'Good.' If you'd like to try it, I can ask again." Her voice dripped with sarcasm.

Normal people. I was definitely not that.

I didn't realize that the two girls from before were now behind me. "I'm sorry. I'm a bit on edge. I've lost someone recently." I regretted saying it as soon as it was out of my mouth. My husband's passing wasn't an excuse and it wasn't a pass to mistreat others.

And then I heard the smallest whisper, "I knew it."

It's so self-satisfied, as if my heartbreak was on their bingo card. There was an urge to glance back, to shoot them a look that would cut them like a dagger but I couldn't bring myself to do it.

I cleared my throat as if that was a doorstop to my bad behavior. "I shouldn't have snapped at you. I'm sorry."

The cashier muttered an, "Okay," and continued to scan items.

I pushed the cart forward and walked to where the items were deposited. Then I pulled out my reusable bag, shoving them in carelessly. Neither of us said anything after that so I kept looking up, hyper-focused on the people in the line behind me. I felt like they were watching me, observing me like an animal in the zoo.

How could they recognize me? Have more TikTok's covered my situation? Did any of them use my picture?

Kelly might have started advertising for her podcast, but how many people could have really tuned into it? The first episode doesn't even have a release date at this point, but maybe she is putting out teasers that are getting traction. If this was the reaction that I was going to get when going out, I had made a crucial mistake. Maybe even fatal.

When I got home, I tossed the frozen dinners into the freezer. Rosco watched me with curiosity as I just stood there with the door open, allowing the cold air to make me feel something, anything. I sifted through the cold boxes. They all looked incredibly unappetizing. There was a good chance I would never eat any of them. I closed the door, disappointed that I had bothered to go out and still didn't have food that I wanted to eat.

I thought to myself, it would probably be weeks and weeks before I could manage the courage to go out in a public space again. Rosco and I sat on the couch as I started to scroll an app for food delivery. Instinctively, my hand went to my mouth. I started chewing on my nails, a habit I had given up in college. Within thirty minutes, enough Chinese food for four arrived. I waited for the text saying my food had been dropped off and then until the driver disappeared down the road. Then I fetched the bag of food, it's heaviness another confirmation that I had over ordered.

While shoving lo mein into my mouth straight from the white and red container as if I hadn't eaten in a week, my phone buzzed. There was a text from Kelly.

> Vacation mode over. Are you free to meet up on Thursday?

I grabbed an egg roll, took a big bite and then gave a thumbs up.

Even the thought of having to go out in the future brought me a tremble of anxiety.

Twenty-Two

Since she lived so close, I walked the few blocks to Kelly's house. She had texted me to let myself in. I knocked and opened the door, peeked in and called for her.

"In here," she said.

I walked toward her recording space. The house was eerily silent. Opening the door to the studio, I found her sitting in her normal spot, her skin tanned from the Las Vegas sun. I noticed she was wearing a light pink eye shadow that brought out her pretty eyes but the smile she normally wore was nowhere to be seen. I thought our last session was a big improvement, even if she was frustrated towards the end. I knew it wasn't exactly what she wanted, but I was not sure why she was acting like this.

"Hello," I greeted her, trying to cut through her cold glare. I approached carefully, the situation not fully making sense to me. "How was the conference?"

"Good." And then she said nothing more. Her pen aggressively tapped on the yellow notepad in front of her.

"Ready?" I said, just trying to break the tension.

She waited for me to sit down across from her. I gave a weak smile but she didn't reciprocate. "You lied to me," she said stone faced.

I was trying to think of what she could be talking about but nothing came to mind. Sure, I had been less than expressive about everything. But that hadn't been a lie. It had been for self-preservation and this was something we worked through last time.

There was silence, thick and stale in the air. I know I should have responded but didn't know what to say. She pushed a worn and hazy photo across the table. I took it and immediately recognized it and the twenty-five little faces. It was my third-grade class photo.

"I don't…"

"Don't play games with me," she said, leaning towards me. I pushed my chair back a bit, uncomfortable with her demeanor. Her eyes flashed anger.

I gulped and the sound pounded loudly in my ear.

"Tell me who that is?"

I looked at where her finger was pointing, feeling like I was in an interrogation room.

"That's me."

Then, her finger slowly glided across the photo. When she stopped, she tapped her pointer finger over and over rapidly. The sound was louder than my heartbeat and her aggressiveness made me wince. "And *that* little girl?" She asked, her voice tight.

My eyes slowly moved in the direction of her finger to the little girl at the end of the row. She was a picture of perfection with a pink floral dress, hair in two neat pigtails, coordinated pink bows at the end of each. Even through the grainy quality, you can see she was beautiful.

"That's Anna."

"And where is Anna now?"

I sighed heavily, averting my gaze as if looking into another time, another place. I was looking back to those days that buzzed with energy, with unplanned playdates that would last all day. They were carefree and filled with laughter—until they weren't.

I dropped my head into my hands and rubbed my temples. I slowly exhaled, feeling the warm breath pass over my lips.

"Where is she?" she repeated, this time her voice hoarser.

I didn't look up. I couldn't look her in the eye—not with what I was about to say. "She's dead."

Memories flooded back to me, drowning me. Memories that had been suppressed deeply and now she had forced them to the surface.

"So, you have another person in your life who has passed away suddenly, and you didn't feel like that was important to mention to me?"

I felt like a trapped animal. I went to stand and I felt a wave of dizziness.

"Brittany, I told you we can't do this if you aren't honest. About every single thing. And you left out this huge part of your life."

The ground beneath me felt unsteady like I was on a ship at sea. "I...I just need a minute," I stammered, my dizziness increasing rapidly as adrenaline coursed through me.

Her face morphed from betrayal to concern to uncertainty.

Without thought, I began to leave the room and then the house. It sounded like she called after me. I couldn't be sure. Her voice was blurred by my breathing that had become difficult to control. It was rapid and forceful. The involuntary motion stung my lungs.

I began to walk more quickly with each step until I was practically running. There was no destination in mind. I was just trying to escape this memory that I thought I had lost decades ago. My mind had been overtaken by something else, like a burglar in the night tossing things around without care. I'm going insane, I told myself. That was the only explanation.

Each step I took felt like it was taking me away from that moment. A moment that awakened something too painful to process. After a while, I realized I had walked so long that I was not exactly familiar with where I was. I'd left my cellphone, keys, everything at her house and was disoriented.

Scanning the street, I saw there was no one around to help me. I slumped onto the curb, feeling the concrete scratching at my bare legs.

My hands were wrapped over my eyes, trying to block out the world so I could focus on what to do next. A car slowly rolled by and I ignored it. Then I heard it reversing, which caused me to jerk my head up. Kelly's red car stopped in front of me.

"Brittany, are you okay?" I just stared at her. "Okay, that was a stupid question. Get in the car." Seeing as I was so disoriented, I didn't feel I had much of a choice. Her demeanor had completely changed and I wondered how she could be talking to me so casually after what had just happened.

I opened the car door and sank into the passenger seat like a moody teenager who'd just got caught sneaking out. The seat was much more comfortable than the curb, so it was worth the temporary embarrassment.

"How did you find me?"

She chuckled softly. "You are like four streets away from my house."

From the passenger's seat I looked at my surroundings and nothing looked familiar. It didn't feel like I could only be four streets away and this disoriented. I looked at her for a long while to see if she was joking. When no smile appeared, it hit me how messed up I was in that moment.

"I shouldn't have hit you with that question, not like that. I'm sorry. I just thought you should have told me about it, but yeah, I see I did that all wrong. Again, I'm sorry."

"It's okay," I heard myself saying. Knowing that it was not okay.

Why do we have this habit of pretending everything is fine? Why can't we scream from the rooftops that we need help, that we aren't okay? Why can't we say I need a hug, a strong drink, some Xanax or everyone to leave me the hell alone?

"Where do we go from here?" she asked when her car was back in her driveway.

"I need a little break. From the podcast, from life."

"I understand. Reach out to me when you are ready to talk again. You'll be okay, right?"

I nodded.

"So, is it okay if I continue the podcast? I can do a few recording sessions on my own giving some background on what happened?"

"Yeah, sure. Do what you need to do." The words came out of my mouth but they weren't what I meant. I didn't know if I would ever be able to talk about all this again, and I didn't know if I wanted anyone else talking about it either.

Twenty-Three

A few weeks went by with only a few texts here and there from Kelly, mostly little updates about what she was doing with the podcast. I spent this time going back and forth on what to do. Every time I thought about the advantages of doing the show—raising reward money, opening a tip line, I would be sucked back to our last conversation. And I knew that we would have to pick up where we left off—the death of Anna.

Kelly reached out to me via text one July night. I was sitting on the porch reading What To Expect When You're Expecting while sipping ice cold lemonade. I was now nearly five months pregnant and was using my free time to get ready for the new arrival.

I held the phone in my hand, staring at it like it was a magic eight ball. The little widget at the top told me there were two-hundred and fifty-one days until this happened again. Just tell me what to do, I begged it silently. And as soon as that thought ran across my mind, I got another message. There is no text, just a link.

The link took me to an article. 'Coffee and Chaos' the headline read. My eyes didn't believe what they were seeing. I scanned the article, taking it all in. There were several local coffee shops in Philly and the Philly suburbs that had been using their storefronts to launder money...and Gritty Grinds was named as one of them. When I saw his name in print: Ian Foster, I propped my hands on my knees and shook my head. This couldn't be happening.

I had never been involved in Ian's business. Of course, I supported him, but I didn't give any help in the day-to-day operations or the behind the scenes. I never had any doubt that everything he did for the shop was in the best interest of the business and for us too. My husband is, was, I corrected, a good guy. He was ethical. He was honest. Kind.

If he had been doing anything unethical, wouldn't I have noticed an influx of money? Our income had remained basically the same over the years. This couldn't be anything more than a hit piece.

I picked up my phone and Kelly answered on the first ring.

"What does this all mean?" I begged her for answers.

"I think Ian was wrapped up in something that could have been a motive."

"I don't think there is a chance in hell that Ian was doing anything wrong. It couldn't have been him. Maybe someone he worked with? What if one of his employees was doing something unethical behind his back? Mike or Charles?"

"It's possible and that would still give someone a motive. Maybe he found out what was happening and was trying to fix it by threatening to get the cops involved. Then someone had to do away with him so they wouldn't get in trouble. Maybe his death wasn't linked to the others and the killer knew your situation and decided that was the perfect day to take care of him—so eyes would turn towards you."

I rubbed my hand across my chin, trying to process it.

"None of this makes sense to me, Kelly. You were a journalist. Shouldn't they have called me for a comment?"

"If Ian was alive, they certainly would have called him. Since you had no link to the business, they might not have been able to use your comment. You are his wife. What would you say other than he didn't do it?"

"Okay, I get that. But they still normally call to get that quote on the record."

"Yeah..." she said, trailing off.

"So, what do we do now?"

"I think this gives enough reason to at least explore this as a motive for his death."

Though she couldn't see it, I was shaking my head. She was heading down the wrong path and we didn't have time to waste on false leads. "If you insist. But it doesn't sit right with me. It doesn't explain my whole story. Do you honestly think Ian's death wasn't connected to the others?"

She clicked her tongue. "I have no idea."

Twenty-Four

Kelly and I began meeting casually. We've temporarily put the project to the side. We needed some level of chemistry in order to tell this story properly. There was too much negativity swirling around the recording studio for it to be successful. For now, we were spending time together in hopes that we could come to some common understanding. So, she started to accompany me on my morning walks with Rosco.

"What have you been working on now?" I asked her.

"I'll be meeting with some podcasters this week, going to see their set up, learning how they edit. I think I jumped into this too quickly and really have a lot to learn if we want it to be perfect. I'm still doing some things behind the scenes for the show too like calling and interviewing people. I should be ready in a few weeks, whenever you are too. Other than that, a little freelance writing. But let's not talk business now."

"Okay, but that's great that those podcasters are willing to take the time to teach you. Hey, I want to show you something," I told her and pulled out my phone. We paused as she flipped through several pictures of the red, white and blue baseball themed nursery accessories. They were unpacked and spread out on my kitchen table. It had arrived a while ago but I hadn't been ready to transition the office to a nursery just yet.

"Such cute stuff!" she squealed. "But what if it's a girl?"

"Girls like baseball!"

"Do you?"

"Not really," I laughed. "But I do like the color scheme. It's fun and exciting. Hopeful, like how Ian felt on the first day of baseball."

She huffed a small laugh. "Opening Day."

"Yeah, that!" I bit my lip nervously. There had been something nagging at me. It started as a small question and had been bombarding my thoughts the more time we spent together. I just had to get it off my chest and ask. I convinced myself to just blurt it out. "Are you afraid to get close to me?"

"Because of the..." and I nodded.

"No, I'm just a podcaster. Doesn't seem like their MO."

"Right, sure," I said, trying to hide that I was a bit disappointed. I assumed we were something akin to friends at this point. Though, if we aren't friends, it keeps her safe. Maybe it was better this way.

She flipped the conversation back to what we were speaking about before.

"How's everything with the baby?" she asked me, her ponytail swinging back and forth like a pendulum as we walked. The teal scrunchie in her hair matched her jogging suit.

I was thankful for the change in topic. "I just had my five-month checkup. I got to hear the baby's heartbeat again."

"That must have been exciting! When will you know if it's a boy or girl?"

"I could have found out already, but I'm not sure if I will or not, though. I'm just praying for a healthy baby, that's all that matters to me. A surprise would be fun." Walking along and chatting felt so strange because it was so normal. "Anyway," I continued. "I ordered all the stuff for the nursery. The items are pretty gender neutral and I feel like that's the biggest reason to want to find out."

"Yeah, for planning purposes. I'd want to know," she said. "Also, I'm pretty type A. I always need as much information as possible."

"I hadn't noticed," I quipped, and she smirked.

"So, when are you going to set it all up? I can't wait to see it all come together."

I raised my eyebrows. "Well...I took all the items out for the photo and then boxed it back up. I felt so overwhelmed by it all so it is currently just sitting in the corner of the office. Definitely before the birth," I joked. The truth was, I was scared. What if I set up the nursery and something happened? How could I ever recover from that? The idea of having a full decorated but never used nursery kept taunting me. That's the real reason I hadn't set it up yet.

She talked to me about gender reveal parties and I was partially listening. I was also scanning the street, as if I was reading it like a book. She started to tell me a funny story about a gender reveal party gone wrong, something she saw on the internet and I heard myself laugh along with her, though I only caught part of the punchline. I didn't bother to mention that most of those were probably staged for views.

"Hey, thank you," I said.

She looked at me with her head tilted.

"I mean, for spending time with me. For making me laugh. I don't recall the last time I laughed," I explained.

Her smile was warm. "It's no problem."

"You remind me of my sister sometimes. She was so easy to talk to. God, I miss her." I sucked in my lower lip, trying not to cry.

Everything kept happening year after year and I never had time to really process anything, to properly grieve. Some part of me wondered if I was like a house of cards, just about to crumble.

Without a word, she stopped walking and turned towards me.

Her arms wrapped around me though the baby bump made it rather awkward. I resisted the urge to pull away. I let her warmth surround me, allowing myself to feel affection. It felt like friendship to me.

She pulled away. "I know this isn't easy but I want you to know, I think you are incredibly brave. To experience what you have and still go about your day. To be willing to share your story so that you can find answers. To get yourself together for the baby."

I looked at my feet as she spoke. The compliment made me uncomfortable. "I mean I barely shower and I look like crap," I said with self-deprecating humor.

"Don't do that. Just take the compliment," she said. "All things considered, you are doing the best you can and I think you are doing a great job."

"Thank you," I said. "I think I'm ready to record again."

"I hope you know that wasn't why I was spending time with you. I just wanted to make sure you were okay."

"I know," I said. Though I hadn't thought about it that way, and now it was all I could think about.

When we parted, we had a plan to meet again in three days. I had three days to dig up all those painful memories.

TWENTY-FIVE

Alone in my room, I let my mind slip back to that place and time that I had locked away. I wasn't sure I'd even be able to recall all or any of the details. Bit by bit, elements start to trickle in and then I could see it, play it in my mind like a movie, like I was right there in that moment.

December 1998

Anna tosses her Powder Puff Girls book bag over the blue plastic chair and sits next to me. I try to nonchalantly kick the My Little Pony book bag that my mom gave me under the desk. It had been my sister Melissa's. No one even liked My Little Pony anymore and I felt like such a baby for having it.

"Good morning," she says brightly, her enthusiasm matched by her bright pink dress. I look at my hand-me-down hunter green dress that has a small hole in the side. Embarrassed, I try to cover it up. Though I couldn't articulate it from my 3rd grade point of view, I know we are different and that it makes me uncomfortable with myself.

"Morning," I say shyly.

We've been best friends since the beginning of first grade and we were lucky enough to be placed in the same third grade class this year. In September, we went to school on the first day and looked for our names on the large chart paper taped to the side of the brick school building.

Anna found both our names first and she shouted, "We are in the same class!" We jumped up and down as we squealed.

When we saw the teacher placed us at the same table, we were overjoyed. When you are that young, being friends for two full school years felt like a lifetime. We used to tell people we'd been friends forever. Drawing out the V like it had three syllables.

"Look what my dad bought me," she says with the level of excitement that can only be made by a child. She carefully pulls out a furry white creature.

"Wow!" I stare at the Furby. "How'd you get that?" She raises her eyebrows up and down with a smirk.

"My dad stood in line overnight for it. It was supposed to be a Christmas gift, but he gave it to me this morning!" Of course, because what Anna wants, Anna gets.

"Wow!" I repeat, in awe that she has one of these. These were like finding a rare gem at this point and every kid wanted one. Parents were literally pushing each other down and running over each other, like bullies on a playground, to get this toy.

Our teacher Ms. Coosin walks by. "Anna, no toys in school!" she scolds.

Anna shoves the Furby into her bag as we giggle. "I'll try to sneak it out to recess," she says leaning over to whisper in my ear and it sends a slight shiver down my spine. I covered my mouth so Ms. Coosin doesn't see that I'm laughing again.

"Cool!" I say quietly, with a big smile. I definitely won't be getting one of these, so playing with it on the playground is about as close to having one as I will get.

When the bell rings at the end of the day, we pack up our things and I say to Anna, "I'll see you tomorrow."

Her dad always picks her up in a dark blue convertible. Both my parents work long hours, so I have to bike to and from school, normally coming back to an empty home.

"My dad said he can't get me today, so he dropped me off this morning with my bike. I can ride home with you! Oh, and he gave me five dollars. We can get candy at Wawa."

I look away. "I don't have any money," I say. She playfully pushes my shoulder.

"I said I have five bucks! That's like enough for five candy bars. I can get you some too."

"Thanks," I mutter, wishing I had my own money. It would feel so cool to be able to walk into a store and buy whatever I wanted.

We start to pedal away from school and the cold air is whipping at our faces. She's in the lead and is chatting away to me. My teeth are chattering so hard that I hear the click, click, clinking in my ears.

"So, I told my dad, if I don't get that Furby, I'll be the only kid in school without one." I can barely hear a word she's saying. The traffic is busy even though it is early afternoon.

"What!" I call up to her as a large truck passes by. The loud engine sound is deafening. She shouts it again but louder.

"But that's not even true!" I shout back. This time it is her turn to not hear. "I'll come up closer," I shout to her.

I pedal up to her left side, hoping we can ride alongside each other and chat on our way to get candy. But I misjudged how narrow the sidewalk was and my handlebars bump into hers. She wobbles, screams and then my memory goes blank.

The next memory I have, I'm sitting at home on my bed clutching a pink teddy bear that I got when I was born. My mother is on one side of me, telling me Anna is in a better place right now. I don't fully understand why she says that. It feels like she is lying.

"The road is not a better place," I said.

My mother pulled back and then tilted her head. "Brittany, she is in heaven now. That's the better place. She is an angel with God. A pretty little angel in a white dress."

"I'm sorry." I wasn't sure if I was apologizing for what I said or what I did.

"It wasn't your fault though," she says to me as she pats my hand. On my other side, sits the worn backpack, a brand new Furby sitting inside that I hope my mother won't find.

"I'm so sorry, sweetheart."

I shrug while swinging my feet up and down. I just want to be alone because I'm embarrassed how badly I want to cry.

"Will you be okay alone?"

I look up at her, shocked. "Why? Where are you going?"

"I'm going to bring a casserole over to Anna's dad. Is that okay?"

I want to tell her not to go but I say nothing. After some silence, my mom gets up to leave. When she reaches the door I say, "Hey mom?"

She turns around, her eyes hopeful. "Yes?"

"Can you give me five bucks for candy tomorrow?" She furrows her brow for just a second and then all expression vanishes from her face.

"Um, yes. I can do that." She pauses a moment and then gives her head a single nod, as if she is giving herself permission to do what she just promised.

She leaves my door ajar and I can see her go to the bathroom sink, open the medicine cabinet and pull something out. My mother opened the tube and spread the red lipstick across her lips. It brightens her whole face.

I get up and shut the door as she is rubbing her lips together. I turn off the light and crawl under the covers. When I hear the loud rumble of her engine, I unzip my backpack and dig out the toy that I clutch. I don't sleep well that night because I'm thinking about what candy I'll buy tomorrow with my own money and how I'll try to show Amanda my new toy.

Kelly pressed record and began with her first prompt. "Tell me about Anna," she said in our next session.

"There isn't anything to tell." My mind went blank and I had no idea what else to say about it.

"It's another death that you are connected to. I think it's important." She leaned in, trying to encourage me to talk. Her eyes bore into me and it made me uncomfortable, I lowered my head, rubbing my forehead vigorously.

"Anna died when I was in third grade. I'm in my mid-thirties now. I don't see what the connection is."

"She's connected to you. We need to talk about it. What happened after she passed away?"

I hadn't talked to anyone about this. The last time I spoke of it was when my mother told me that Anna died, sitting on my bed all those years ago. Since then, it had been locked away and buried, like a time capsule. "We, uh, we moved. I think a few months later. From Blackwood to Cherry Hill. I've been here ever since." I added the last part, though she doesn't care about that tidbit now.

"Why did you move so suddenly?"

"My family was worried. I had blocked the memory out of my mind. I had zero recollection of it for years and years after. For everyone else, it was a painful mark on their young lives. When kids would ask me about it, they would tease me, yell at me, accuse me of doing something terrible. I was starting to withdraw into myself—not talking to anyone, not doing my schoolwork, not really caring about much of anything."

A glimpse of that time came back to me. "After Anna's passing, I was home for a week or so with my family, though no one talked about what had happened. When I finally went back to school, I was struggling, but not realizing the torment that awaited me. Kids bombarded me with questions. I had no answer for them. I had blocked it all out. But they took it as a guilty admission. So, they kept asking and asking questions that increasingly made me feel like I had some part in it."

"Kids can be so cruel. I'm so sorry." She sounded sympathetic but I couldn't be sure if it was an act for the recording or a genuine reaction.

I didn't know what to say. The silence was unsettling as she waited for more of the story while I wanted to run away from the whole thing.

"So, what happened next?" she prompted.

"We were in a new house two or three months after she passed. We literally never talked about it again. My family was like that." We were a family with tensions, frustrations, secrets all bottled up.

"You were best friends for about two years, right? Were your families close?"

"No, not really...they were...well, they were in different circles," I told her as I shifted in my seat.

I'm not sure why it was so difficult for me to try to explain this to her. I'm a grown adult and can't say the simple truth—that I grew up poor and Anna was wealthy. Somehow, I still felt that sting of embarrassment and shame. She nodded as if she understood.

"So, you're saying you didn't talk about it, but did it change your family dynamic in any way?"

"I felt like my dad became more protective, more involved. I'm not a parent yet but I imagine when something like that happens you become very worried for your own child and I think he thought he could lose me at any moment."

"What about your mom? Was she overprotective too?"

"No."

Kelly mouthed "Say more" to me.

So, I continued. "No, my mother was actually more distant. They took opposite approaches. My dad was always around but my mother found other activities outside the house to keep her busy." I prayed she didn't ask me why I thought that was. I'm not a therapist. Luckily, she moved on to a new topic.

"Did you ever wonder what happened after her passing? To her family?" There is something in her voice that was different as she asked this, but I was unsure of what she was trying to hint at.

"No, like I said, I really had no memory of it. Obviously, I feel bad for them. It must have been incredibly difficult for them."

She shook her head. Her eyes began to glisten, as they rimmed with tears. Kelly leaned over and grabbed a tissue from the center of the table to wipe her cheeks. Her sudden show of emotions confused me.

"You have no idea," she croaked out.

"What does that mean?" I felt a slight tremor in my hands and I slid them under my thighs so she didn't notice.

"Anna's mom was sick. Did you know that?"

"No, I know her dad took care of her a lot more than her mother did, which wasn't as common back then as it is now. As a kid, I noticed it but didn't think much of it. But Amanda and I did tease her about being a daddy's girl. It was all in good fun though. She never said anything about her mother being sick. What was wrong with her?"

"She had a pretty aggressive form of cancer. She passed away a few weeks after her daughter's death. People I spoke to said the heartbreak took her early."

I wondered if it would do the same for me.

"Wait, you said you spoke to people...from Anna's family?"

"Yes."

My mind started to pop off thoughts like fireworks...

Pop - They will say you were so careless.

Pop - They said you were jealous of her. So pretty, so bubbly.

Pop - They called you a nasty little girl.

Pop - They probably said you did it on purpose.

I started speaking just to clear my mind of the racing thoughts. "I'm really surprised by this news. God, I had no idea. I'm so sorry. What happened after that?"

"Well, then it was just her father. He lost his whole family in a single season. They said he drank heavily to cope. It didn't work.

He, um, well he couldn't continue on," she said, her voice trailing off at the end.

I gasped and covered my shaking hand over my mouth. "You don't mean he...?"

She gulped and let out a small sound of affirmation.

"That's awful."

"I know. It's a tragic story. I suppose it's a good thing your family moved away. You wouldn't have wanted to be growing up surrounded by that story."

It would have been this darkness hanging over me, following me like a shadow. I couldn't imagine growing up in a town always being thought of as the girl who killed her friend. Moving gave us a fresh start where I could be a carefree child, as opposed to the girl rumored to have caused her friend's death.

"Why are you telling me all of this?"

"Don't you see?" She looked at me as if I didn't have two brain cells to rub together. I shook my head.

She took out a photo of Anna and I, then placed it before me. "Your story and Anna's story are connected. Because you—" She paused before finishing her thought, "were both there when she died." I looked down at the photo as I felt my heart shrivel like a raisin.

"You were going to say I caused it! I didn't! I was a small child."

I turned away from her and the photo. I couldn't even look at this woman, who pulled these memories from me that had been buried so deep that I wasn't even aware they existed. My chest felt tight, like someone was sitting on top of me. It was hard to catch a breath. When I did take in air, it wasn't enough and I continued to inhale, hungry to fill my lungs.

"No, I was going to say that it seems like there has to be a link to what happened to her family and to yours. This moment in time triggered so much tragedy for you both."

I shook my head rapidly. My head was screaming no, no, no but nothing came out of my mouth. Kelly stood up, turned off the recording and came over to me. Shit, I forgot she was recording all this. The realization that she has audio of my reaction to everything was alarming. How did I come off in these clips? Would people find me genuine and sympathetic?

I felt her hand on my shoulder, icy cold. "It wasn't your fault," she said gently. When I didn't respond, she said, "Let's take a break. I'll go make you a coffee. Decaf?"

I nodded.

I sat there, I don't know how long. Just letting the thoughts and the feelings wash over me. They were all too much. At some point, I got up, creeping past the kitchen as the coffee started to brew. I slipped my shoes back on at the front door and saw myself out without a word. The point of exposing my feelings and trauma to this podcast was to give me answers. Now I just had more questions, more feelings, more trauma.

Twenty-Six

Where did you go?

Followed by a series of other unread texts sat in my inbox. It was going to be awhile before I was able to reach out to Kelly. Though I knew I would need to resume our recordings, I was not emotionally ready for that. I picked up the phone, clicked the saved number and waited for an answer.

"Morning. Gritty grinds. Erol speaking. How can I help you?" I heard the familiar sounds in the background. Coffee beans being ground, the soothing sound of coffee being brewed, people ordering their lattes, soft unrecognizable chatter in the background.

"It's Brittany. Can I speak to Mike?"

"Sure. Hold on."

Mike picked up the phone. "Mike speaking."

"Hi, it's Brittany."

"Oh. Oh. Okay." and then I heard the familiar sounds grow fainter. "Yeah, one second. Let me just get to the back room." After I heard the door shut, he seemed to compose himself. "Hi, Brittany. How are you holding up?"

"Ebbing between disbelief and grief."

"I'm so sorry." He said flatly.

"Did Charles get a hold of you? He said awhile back that he needed some documents."

"Yeah, it's all good."

"Okay, good. Listen, I'm calling because—"

"This isn't about that shitty article, right? It was total bullshit." His voice quickly rose to anger and I felt the need to calm him down.

"No, no, absolutely not. I thought it was BS too. I wanted to stop by the shop to talk to you in person."

I wasn't ready to be seen in public, especially not a place that I would be recognized. However, I had no choice. The inheritance I got from my parents' passing was nearly gone and for the past six months Mike had sent small biweekly checks. With my bank account in the low thousands and no foreseeable income, I needed to look into finally settling Ian's estate.

"Of course. You're welcome at any time. You know that, right?"

"Yeah. Thanks. I'm not sure how to say this but I didn't get Ian's paycheck this week. Can you look into it?"

"Yeah, I'll do that later today. Might take me some time though."

"Sure. I understand. It's just hard suddenly having one income."

"I understand, Listen I gotta—"

"Wait!" I said loudly, so he didn't hang up. "That's not the only thing. Pretty soon we will have to work out what happens to the shop since Ian didn't have a will. I hope we can split this fairly."

I heard him exhale. "Brittany...Ian had a will."

My ears and brain must have been playing tricks on me because I couldn't have heard what I thought I heard. Neither Ian nor I had a will. We talked about it a few times but thought it was pointless at this time in our lives. That's what we always said, but

I think some part of us didn't want to think about the other one's passing.

When we have kids we will make one, we'd say. At that point, it was just the two of us, so all our assets would just go to the other person.

"That's impossible. Ian and I always talked about how we should draft one but never got around to it. He did not have a will," I said forcefully.

"When he decided to expand to more than one shop, he made me an equal business partner. One of the first things our lawyer suggested was to get wills drafted so that the business was protected if something happened to either one of us. Charles has a copy of it too." I heard him typing rapidly, and I could envision him sitting there so casually, so self-assured.

"Mike, I'm sorry. I, uh, have to go. I'll get back to you soon." I didn't know how to take this news and getting off the line as quickly as possible seemed the best way not to say something stupid that I'd regret. I needed a moment to process this.

I hung up and let the phone slip from my hand. My legs felt weak and I wobbled to the couch before they fully let out. Either my husband was hiding things from me or Mike was taking advantage of his death. Then my body froze. What if he wasn't taking advantage of his death...but was the cause of it.

Twenty-Seven

I went into our shared office space. The nursery items that were still boxed up sat in the corner. Logically, it made no sense that they were still in boxes. But grief and fear aren't logical. Once the nursery was set, it would be there to welcome a baby and I couldn't get past the intrusive thoughts that kept screaming at me, "What if you don't bring home a baby?" I shuddered at the thought.

In the back corner of the room, Ian had a large cherry oak desk. I always thought it was a little grand and over the top, given he mostly worked in small backrooms at the different coffee shops. But we were DINKs (Double income, no kids) so we could afford the nicer things, even when they weren't necessary.

"We gotta spend our money somehow," he would always joke when we bought something we didn't need.

I opened each drawer, carefully flipping through the papers, receipts, pens and other junk. There were documents from different coffee farms he had visited, trying to find the best beans to sell his customers. There was a lot of paperwork from vendors. Nothing special.

When I got to the last drawer, I pulled and was met with resistance. I tugged harder, assuming it was jammed. No luck. Something was telling me I needed to get into this drawer. I searched for a key in the kitchen junk drawers, his work bag and the night-stands. No luck. I'd have to break into it. But was I really going to crack open my husband's desk, destroy one of the few things I had left of him?

That felt all wrong. For now, I left it. Having a will is not unheard of, especially when you are in a joint business venture. What wasn't normal was that he never mentioned Mike having an equal share in the business. And what about Charles? Mike said he had made him whole. Was he lying? Maybe Ian did make a will and it just slipped his mind to tell me. Maybe he thought of a will between us was different than a will centered around his business.

In the back of my mind I heard, *What if Mike needed to get Ian out of the picture, took advantage of this connection and orchestrated his death to fall on this day?*

It wasn't out of the realm of possibility. If he wanted to do him harm, that day was the perfect day, so it would be lumped in with all the others.

Focusing on Ian seemed like I was missing the big picture here. All of these deaths had to be connected. There was no way that each of these were separate incidents so I needed to focus on the connection. What link was there between Ian, my parents, my best friend, my sister and my childhood friend...other than me?

After a restless night, the sun rose on a new day, I jumped up from my bed as a loud knock on the front door startled me, sending my heart into a frenzy. As I made my way to the door, Rosco followed behind me. I peered through the peephole. Standing there was a young man, a large envelope in his hand. "Yes?" I shouted through the door.

"I'm looking for a Brittany Foster. I have certified mail for her."

"Hold it up to the door," I commanded.

It was exhausting to be so suspicious of everyone around me.

He briefly rolled his eyes and I decided he was more likely a frustrated mail worker than a hitman. My name was clearly printed on the manila envelope so I slowly opened the door.

After signing the document, I opened the envelope. I held my breath as I pulled out the papers. It was a copy of the will that Mike had told me about leaving full ownership of Gritty Grinds to him. Leaving me with zero ownership of the company, and a major loss of my income.

When I asked Mike about the paycheck, he said he was looking into it, but it seemed he was intentionally not paying. He strung me along for six months and then cut me off. Now I'd have to worry about paying the mortgage on my own, on top of everything else. I officially had no income, a dwindling inheritance and a baby on the way.

Word by word, I examined the document. There wasn't any mention of Charles either. How could he leave everything to one partner and not the other? And Mike said he knew about it, so Charles agreed to be completely cut out of something he helped to build after taking some parting check from Mike? The whole thing was baffling.

I could understand why Ian wanted to write a will and why the business would go to his partner since I had zero experience running a coffee shop. Nor did I have the time to run one given I had my own job, at least I had a job when this was written. What I didn't understand was why he didn't let me know that. Why didn't he tell me that if anything happened to him, I'd be left with half our income and all our bills? He had to know that I couldn't keep all this up on my own. He had to know that while I couldn't run the business day to day, that giving up full financial stake in it made no sense.

I was convinced Ian didn't know about this will either. It was possible that Mike drafted this fake document once Ian passed in order to take the business all for himself. This way he wouldn't have to share any of the profits. Or maybe there were more sinister reasons for all this. I couldn't push that thought out of my head.

. . .

Sitting at Ian's desk, I ran my hand over the smoothly polished wood and closed my eyes. Then, I opened them, took a deep breath and clicked until I was on Google. My gaze was towards the screen, but my mind was assaulting me with one thought after another, so I saw nothing. I hit my cheeks to snap myself out of it. I typed in NJ...And then what? Death Laws? Spouse will rights? I erased it and typed; *Can a husband cut his wife out of the will?* Endless articles popped up, after sifting through a few, the jargon was just too much for my overwhelmed brain.

It was clear that I needed to seek professional help on this...I probably needed professional help with a lot of things.

Twenty-Eight

The midsummer heat and my changing body, made walking Rosco difficult. We walked along the sidewalk slowly and I marveled at how intuitive this creature was. His boundless energy was reigned in for my benefit as he slowed his pace to stay right at my side. I wanted to reach down and hug him but knew that the likelihood of being able to get back up wasn't 100%.

My phone pinged and I opened it up to see a message from Kelly. She had been messaging me with updates since the last time we met up and it seemed like she was making good progress. She had three sponsors lined up and was trying to gain a following on different social media platforms.

> The promos are in...Check them out and let me know what you think.

I turned to Rosco, "Come on boy. Let's head home and check these out." I could feel my back start to tighten and was eager to sit down to look these over.

As we rounded the corner to the condo, my neighbor was out,

planting yellow marigolds on the pathway to our doors. "Hi, Betty," I said, praying I recalled her name correctly.

"Hello dear!"

I silently let out a sigh of relief that I used the right name. Betty's eyes went to my illuminated phone. A text from Kelly had come in and my screen filled with the image she sent me, a thumbnail for the podcast that featured her smiling face.

"Oh, I know her," she said.

"You do?" I asked, squeezing my eyebrows together.

"Yes, she came by my house a few weeks ago asking about you."

I puffed out my cheeks and let the air out slowly. "Let me just put my dog inside. Be right back." I cracked open the door and let him in. "So, what did she want to know?" I asked, putting my hand on my now aching back.

She titled her watering can above the newly planted flowers. "Oh, not much. She was just asking what I think about you! And I said I didn't know you very well but that I thought you were lovely," she said, smiling sweetly.

"Did she ask anything else?"

Betty tapped on her chin, leaving a small speck of dirty there and looked up. "No, not that I can remember."

"Okay, thanks for letting me know. The flowers look beautiful, by the way. I better go in," I said, resting my hand on my stomach.

"Yes, dear. It's much too hot to be out here in your condition. Go drink some water!"

We said our goodbyes and she turned back to her flowers. Inside the condo, the AC provided immediate relief from the heat. With a cup of ice water in my hands, I carefully lowered myself onto the couch with a groan and Rosco joined me.

He looked at me and I told him, "We need to figure out what the hell is going on with this podcast." I opened my phone and looked over what she sent me. In bright orange font it said, 'Proxy

Black Widow speaks for the first time.' My fingers couldn't text fast enough, "No way." I shut the phone off, not wanting to talk to her or anyone else for a while.

TWENTY-NINE

arly one morning there was a chime at my door. I decided to ignore it and tossed the comforter over my head. I was now six and a half months pregnant and trying to get out of bed and walk, waddle rather, to the door was just too much effort. The bell chimed again. I groaned, slipped my feet into my fuzzy slippers and made my way to the door. Through the peephole I saw a woman, she was baby faced and carrying a cardboard box. Her green eyes looking back and forth as she waited. The box was large but looked light judging by the ease she seemed to be carrying it.

"Can I help you?" I shouted through the door. I heard Rosco jump off the bed and start to make his way toward the door.

"I'm looking for a Brittany Foster."

"Who's asking for her?" Rosco looked up at me, assessing the situation. "It's okay boy," I whispered to him and he settled a bit.

"I'm Ian's stepsister."

That didn't track at all and it immediately put me on guard. Ian didn't have siblings. As far as I knew, he had no family. He lost his parents when he was younger and was raised by a grandmother who also passed away. It was one of the things he struggled with, which was why I think he would have been so excited about the unexpected news of our baby. That thought made my hand go to my stomach as I rested it on top of my baby bump.

"I have some of his things, from when he was a child. I wanted to give them to you," she shouted back through the door. "It's nothing big, but they were his and, well, you should have them." Her voice weakened and she shifted a bit to get a better hold on the box.

At this point, I trusted no one. I went into amateur spy mode. Examining her face, I didn't see a resemblance to Ian's sharp features. She looked about his age, early forties, but had a button nose and a rounded chin.

"Where did Ian grow up?"

"Jersey City."

"Where did he go to college?"

"Rowan."

Hmmm... maybe those tidbits were in his obituary or could be easily found online.

"What's his favorite movie?"

"The Big Lebowski...but if he was drinking, Legally Blonde."

I snorted. That was true and definitely wasn't common knowledge. I smiled thinking of him doing the 'pop and snap' after a few Irish car bombs. God, I missed him and the way we laughed so easily together.

Okay, so she knew that tidbit. I was starting to let my guard down and also screaming through the door was starting to make my voice hoarse.

I opened it up just a crack, but still left the chain latched.

"Show me what's in the box," I commanded.

She placed it on the ground and opened the flaps. There were yearbooks from schools he attended resting on top of a blanket and some other small items. That's all I could see. She looked up at me, her small smile creating wrinkles around her eyes and mouth.

I unlatched the chain and motioned for her to come in. As I had been doing so often, I had my hand resting on my stomach.

Her eyes went wide as she noticed the baby bump. She saw the change in my expression and I moved my hand to my hip.

"Um...are you?"

I nodded slowly.

"Oh, fuck."

"Yeah."

She was scowling now. "I need a moment."

"Here, come on in," I said.

She came in, put the box down and then sat. She placed her head in her hands and started to cry. I was not sure what to do with this stranger crying in my living room. I looked away uncomfortably but was drawn back when I heard her gasping for air.

"Are you okay?"

She couldn't respond, she was hyperventilating. She had cupped her hands over her mouth in an attempt to steady her breathing.

Momentarily, I was trying to figure out what to do.

I kept my eyes on her while going to grab a paper bag from the kitchen. I handed it to her. As she was loudly heaving in and out, I rubbed her back as I cooed, "You're okay. Everything is okay."

Once her breathing calmed, she spoke. "Sorry, I just wasn't expecting that. It's just so tragic for Ian, ya know?"

"Yeah," I said simply, thinking it's rather tragic for me and the baby too.

I watched her carefully as she sat down on the couch. She was looking around the room, noticing things on the wall.

"You have a nice home," she said to me.

"This is not my home."

She wrinkled her face in confusion.

"A home is where you spend time with the people you love, a place that brings you comfort. This is just a place I eat and sleep," I said flatly.

She shifted on the couch, clearly unaware how to respond.

I was still not fully accepting this situation but she looked like the girl next door. She had to be harmless, right?

"Ian didn't tell me he had any siblings."

"I'm his stepsister. We didn't grow up together so we'd see each other just a few times a year when we were little." Her hands were resting on her lap and she seemed mildly uncomfortable. As I sat across from her, her face did start to look familiar. She must have been at the funeral, one of the many people I greeted but had little recollection of afterwards.

"He didn't tell me he had one of those either. So clearly you weren't very close but you have his things?"

"I was cleaning out his grandmother's storage space and found them. I thought you'd want them." Her bottom lip started to quiver and her eyes began to dampen in the corners.

I decided to back off my investigation.

"So how often did you two see each other?"

"We ended up going to the same college together so daily at that point in our lives. We stayed close for a while but you know how things get busy after college. A few years ago, I moved up to North Jersey and we just fell out of touch."

Something didn't sit right though. "If you haven't talked in years, how did you find out about the funeral? How did you know about his things in storage?"

She looked off to the side. "Mike called me."

What the hell? I cocked my head to the side and before I could respond she spoke. "When Ian started Gritty Grinds right out of college, we were still really close then. I helped him with the logo. I'm a graphic designer. So, I was at a few of their early meetings. Mike and I...well, we went on a few dates. But that's ancient history."

I eyed the box curious as to what was in it but I wanted to be alone when I went through it all. I needed time to process everything she told me and awkwardly changed the topic.

"I see. So, what was Ian like as a kid?" I realized I wanted to sit with her and hear about Ian for as long as she was willing to stay with me. For her to give me pieces of him that I never got. When you are talking about, reminiscing about someone, it's as if they are there for a split second.

"Silly. Never liked to be the center of attention but when he was, he hammed it up." We smiled and then looked away from each other, lost in our own memories. "I should probably go. I didn't mean to come into your space and then nearly have a panic attack. Not the best introduction."

I muttered some words of comfort, telling her not to worry about it. She motioned toward the box. "I know nothing brings him back, but hopefully his belongings can bring you some peace." She gulped and pulled her lips into a sad smile.

Part of me wanted her to leave, part of me wanted to ask for her number, say we should meet up so she can tell me stories about Ian. She was my only connection to him. But she was out the door before I could decide what to do.

I went to the window just in time to see her car pulling away. I jotted down the make but had no idea what model it was. I added that she had a Pennsylvania license plate despite the fact that she said she lived in North Jersey. Who was the stranger I had just let in my home?

The box she left sat where she placed it. I traced the rim, both wanting to dive in and not wanting to touch it at all. Rosco came over and sniffed at the box, then sat beside me. There was this internal conflict between wanting to be immersed in something that was his but also being so scared of the pain that it would bring. Why was everything about grief two different extremes? I patted his head. "Should we open it?" He licked my hand in response. I took that as a yes.

This old, tattered, box was like a treasure chest just sitting on my floor, waiting for me to peer inside. As I pulled back the flaps, Rosco stood up and looked inside with me, probably hoping to find some new toy. I took out Ian's yearbooks and read the messages that old classmates left. Most were hastily scribbled. The back pages were filled with thoughtless notes: *have a good summer!* But some made me laugh. I imagined a younger version of him, standing there peering over the book as someone jotted down their message. Something about holding an object he held made me feel like I was linked to him, even if it was momentary. It calmed all my anxiety and I was thankful that she took the time to bring me these things.

Then I pulled out the blanket and wrapped it around me. I inhaled but rather than his signature scent, it smelled musty. The scent was overwhelming and I could feel my throat constrict as I gagged. The burning pressure rose in my chest and I rushed to the bathroom. I hurled myself over the toilet and threw up.

After my stomach settled, I left the bathroom to return to the box. I delicately picked up the blanket, holding it as far away as possible and tossed it back into the cardboard container. I decided to move the box to our balcony to let it air out a bit. My sense of smell was heightened from the pregnancy and I would have to wait for the smells to subside before looking through his things again.

THIRTY

y phone rang, causing me to jump. "Hello?"

"Brittany? Yeah, it's me, Sal."

My attorney. Of course, he was returning my phone call about the will. "Did you find out anything?"

"I've had a chance to review the document. It looks legitimate." He stopped talking and I waited for him to tell me more. "But, Brittany, are you sure you didn't talk about this together? You don't have a copy anywhere in your home?"

My mind had been clouded with grief but I'm pretty sure I'd remember something like that. "No, we didn't. I've searched everywhere." Then I recalled the one place I hadn't looked. "There is a drawer in his desk that's locked. I haven't been able to get into it."

"You are a creative girl. I'm sure you can figure out a way."

"Sure, yeah. I'll, uh, break into it."

"Good girl." My skin crawled at the comment.

I quickly said goodbye, ruminating over the fact that about two decades had passed since I was last called a girl.

Ian had a few tools in the hallway closet. I don't think I ever saw him use one but for some strange reason, he had a large collection. They were sitting all the way at the top. The box was heavy and I worried about trying to pull it off the high shelf. Could I hurt the baby by lifting this? Instead, I opted to grab a small stool, and rummaged through until I found a hammer.

I walked quickly, with wide strides, to his office. I was eager to get this over with, because I felt like I was betraying him by damaging his desk. Once I destroyed the locked drawers, I'd have to get rid of the whole desk. And so would begin the first step in cleansing him out of my life.

Standing in front of the desk, I slowly panned the room. For one more moment, I wanted to take it all in. His things. Our shared space. The life we had. The boxes of nursery items still waiting patiently in the corner to be unpacked. It was time I told myself.

My body didn't possess a single handy bone so I was not sure how to even go about this. I used the opposite side of the hammer (does it even have a name?) to try to pry open the drawer. It caused knicks and scratches in the wood, but it was still firmly locked.

Gazing towards the sky, as if he was looking down at this event, I whispered, "I'm sorry. But I promise you'll like what I do with the room."

Tears ran down my cheeks as I pulled the hammer back and then propelled it forward with all my strength. When it collided with the wood, my eyes were closed, and the cracking sound stabbed at my heart. I struck over and over again, surprised that the release of pent-up energy was a huge relief.

When I opened my eyes, there was a big, jagged hole, exposing the inside of the drawer. I used my hands to pull away at the wood that remained, careful not to get a splinter. I peered inside, frowning deeply. There was nothing in there. Not a single paper, nor pen in a drawer he deemed important enough to lock. The drawer was completely empty as if someone had already gotten there before me.

Not eager to speak to Sal for the second time in a day, I shot him a text.

> It wasn't in there. Now what?

> I'll have to go talk to his partner Mike. We need more answers about when this will was created and who was present. I'll try to get there by the end of the week.

> Thank you. Keep me posted.

> Will do.

I headed to my bedroom and put the phone in my nightstand.

I needed a moment to disconnect. I turned on reruns of Always Sunny in Philadelphia, a show we used to watch together because it was so close to home. With each crazy antic the characters got into, there was only my tired laughter in response which slowly tapered off as the episode went on. This wasn't enjoyable without him. After one show, I turned it off and decided it was time to go to bed.

This happened often. I would find something that we used to do together and think if I do it now, it will provide comfort. Then it hit differently and either leaves me frustrated, dissatisfied or angry. I would abandon it but never seem to learn my lesson, trying things over and over in an effort to find elusive comfort.

I laid under my covers, looking up at the ceiling and thinking about what I had just done. Destroyed his things, violated his trust. It made me hope there wasn't an afterlife so he wouldn't know what I did. Then I thought that if that was true, I'd never see him again. Maybe I did wish there was an afterlife so I could explain myself and ask forgiveness. I wasn't sure. There were no good answers in grief.

THIRTY-ONE

I awoke early as the sun's rays crept past my curtains. Sleeping and pregnancy don't mix well. My ever-growing stomach causes me to toss and turn, never finding a comfortable position. The baby's pressure causes me to often wake from acid reflux and lately I've been getting painful Charlie horses in my leg.

Despite the fact that they say you shouldn't have coffee while pregnant, I figured a half-caf would be fine once in a while. I just needed a little pick me up to get me through the day. There was a new coffee shop not too far from my house and I decided to walk there.

It was my first time out since the grocery store incident. Despite how traumatizing it was, I felt ready. Maybe it was less about being ready and more about going stir-crazy. Either way, being outside and breathing fresh air was invigorating.

It was the last weeks of summer and the temperature was quickly rising. Cotton candy clouds floated above me. I wanted an iced coffee, but wasn't sure which summer specialty drinks they had. I was excited to look at the menu but my favorite was the fall drink menu that would hit in a few weeks.

I placed my order, a coconut and chocolate flavored iced latte and waited. As I looked around, everyone went about their business and I felt comfortable in public for the first time in a long time. I threw a few dollars into the tip jar and took my coffee to go. I began to walk briskly back home as the flavor hit my tongue. A gentle breeze kissed my face. I thought to myself that everything was perfect.

Perfect.

A wave of guilt rushed over me. I shouldn't have perfect moments. I'd lost my husband nearly seven months ago, my soulmate. There should be no happiness without him, at least not this soon. My grief was a self-inflicted prison and I didn't want to be let out, because freedom felt like disrespect. To him, to what we had, to the vows that I had made.

I continued my walk, bowing my head. The conditions around me were still the same but now I viewed them as an injustice. Why was the world still so beautiful without him here? I wanted the sky to remain cloudy without him. I wanted the birds to stop singing without him. I wanted sounds, smells, and tastes to dim because he wasn't there to enjoy them. My world stopped, why didn't everyone else's?

The rest of the walk home, I thought unkind things about myself. You didn't love him enough. You didn't protect him. You don't deserve to be happy.

I dumped the practically full coffee in the trash and crawled into my bed, Rosco joining me moments later. I wrapped the covers around me, creating my own cocoon. Through a lullaby of self-deprecation, I fell asleep quickly, though it was not even noon yet.

Thirty-Two

When I woke up, I reached for my phone, the little icon in the top saying there were two-hundred and four days until tragedy struck again. I dialed Kelly, thinking about what Betty had told me about her coming around. I wasn't sure if I should be going to her with this information but it was too late because she picked up on the first ring. I heard someone in the background talking to her, a deep voice.

"Is this a bad time?"

I heard her shush whoever was there. "No, what's up?"

"Something strange happened last week. Someone stopped by claiming to be Ian's stepsister. But Ian never said he had any siblings." I left out the part about the box for now, unsure what I was ready to reveal about that.

"Oh lord, did you talk with her?"

"Yeah. She was here for, like, forty minutes."

"Here? Like you let her into your house?"

"Yeah..." I said hesitantly. "Why?"

I heard her sigh heavily. "I'm not trying to overstep my bounds...but shouldn't you be careful?"

"It's fine." I said, trying to hide my embarrassment. "She was sweet. A little emotional but it was fine." I definitely needed to be careful. Letting a stranger into my home was beyond stupid. "Listen, I want to meet with you and see if we can figure out who she is."

"I've got just the person," she replied cheerfully. "How's this weekend?"

Soon I would find out that we couldn't wait that long.

THIRTY-THREE

The box had been sitting out on my deck for the last few nights, which I was hoping would be enough time to have the smells disappear—or at least have faded away to the point that it didn't make me sick. It would be nice to take his blanket and put it on our bed. I peered through the sliding glass window and thought it was time to bring it in. I lifted the light box and jostled it a bit trying to readjust so I had a better grip on it. When I did, I heard a sound from inside the box. It was muffled so I couldn't make it out.

"Ready to see what's inside?" I asked Rosco.

When I laid the box down in the middle of our living room, Rosco and I simultaneously sniffed. The smell seemed to have dissipated. I took out the items one by one, carefully. The yearbooks, a small trophy from a day camp in the pine barrens that said, 'best swimmer', the light blue blanket, some t-shirts from college events and then there was only one thing left at the bottom of the box—the source of the muffled noise.

I stared in disbelief. This can't be, I thought to myself. I rubbed my eyes with balled fists as if in a cartoon and looked again. It was still there, looking back at me.

A small white Furby, fur worn from age.

Its eyelids were open, showing off its big, round eyes. Creepy, haunting eyes.

I flipped it over and saw the small crimson dots caked on the white fuzz.

"No, no, no, no," I cried out.

I dropped it to the floor and as it hit the ground with a thud, it started speaking again. This time I heard it clearly.

"Hello Brittany."

I backed away quickly, crab crawling until I could get to my feet, urgently trying to get as far from it as possible.

I know this small toy, I thought to myself.

It was Anna's.

THIRTY-FOUR

"I don't understand," I repeated to myself.

Who was the woman that left this box at my house? Why did she have some of Ian's things? Why did she have this toy? Who changed the batteries in this twenty-year-old toy, giving life to something that should have died years ago?

I felt even stupider for letting her into my home.

It occurred to me that it had been sitting outside for a week and anyone could have put it there. Obviously, this woman couldn't have had my friend's childhood toy, right? No. Someone was stalking me. Someone was leaving me clues about what they knew.

My eyes couldn't focus and I was overcome with dizziness. I closed them to cease the unsettling sensation.

When I composed myself, I picked up the toy, holding it as far away from me as possible, as if it was toxic. After tossing it into the hall closet and slamming the door, I grabbed my phone and called Kelly.

"Hello?" came an upbeat voice.

"I need you to come over right now." My voice was deep, desperate, and panicked.

"Brittany? What's wrong? Is everyone...okay?"

"No one is hurt but I'm not okay. I need your help. It's about the lady I just told you about."

"I can be there in like 15 minutes. I've got the private investigator that I've been working with here. Is it okay if he comes along?"

"Um, sure. I guess." I really wasn't eager to have another stranger in my home.

Kelly entered my house with a man at her side. She introduced him as her investigator partner, Hank. "This is the person I was telling you about who can help us figure out who came to your house."

I nodded.

Hank had a black beard that was trimmed close to his face and dressed like he was twenty years younger than he clearly was. Rosco sat staring at him. I hadn't had time to figure out what they were to each other; other than he helped with the research aspect of the podcast.

As they walked into the main room, I suddenly became conscious of how incredibly messy this space had become. I picked up several cups, filled with various liquids and tossed them into the sink. As they sat, I picked up as many wrappers as I could grab and tossed them too.

"Brittany, it's okay. We know you have a lot going on," she said.

My cheeks flushed from embarrassment but I joined them on the couch even though I hadn't tidied up everywhere.

"So, what's going on?" Kelly asked.

I eyed Hank and he got up from the couch, extending his hand and I shook it. "Sorry, we didn't do a proper intro. I'm Hank. I'm the private investigator helping with the podcast and..." he looked back at Kelly. "...her boyfriend."

Kelly looked up at me shyly, gauging my reaction. "I mean, we are just sorta dating."

Hank shrugged but didn't refute her.

"So back to what you were saying, tell us what's going on," Kelly said, clearly wanting to change the subject.

I gave them the whole backstory on how I met this woman, what she dropped off and what happened with the blanket. I did not mention the item that had caused me to call them in a panic. Hank took notes on a small pocket notepad as I spoke.

I showed them the footage from the ring camera. Hank downloaded it to his phone and promised me he would figure out who she was.

"Who she is? That's only one part of the puzzle. What about why she lied to me? Why she came into my home? How she had access to Ian's things?"

He shrugged for the second time and I started to doubt his competency. "I know. But it's a start. Once we figure out who she is, we can decide what the next move needs to be."

It suddenly felt stifling hot. I rubbed my hand over my forehead. "Okay...let's start there," I said, because I really didn't have any other choice. But I was nervous. There were too many unanswered questions and I didn't feel safe here. It made me want to run away from this place, which was an impulsive reaction and probably fruitless. I wasn't not sure if I'd feel safe anywhere.

Hank must have picked up on my anxiety because despite the fact that he looked like he'd be rough around the edges, he leaned in and said, "We are going to do everything we can to figure all this out for you so you can get back to feeling secure again. You deserve that."

Kelly nodded her head as he spoke.

I knew he was right, but sometimes I didn't feel like I deserved anything.

Despite my original doubts, Hank must be a pro at what he does because it wasn't even twenty-four hours before the two of them were back at my front door ringing the bell.

"Sit down," Kelly commanded.

"We've got some news." Hank backed her up.

Hank tossed a manilla folder onto the table. I flipped through the printouts, growing more confused. There were printouts from a Facebook page, dating from a decade before. There was Ian, with his supposed stepsister—but they didn't look like siblings posing for a photo. His arm was across her waist, bringing her close so their hips touched. She's looking at him in a way that the emotion jumped off the page. One thing was clear from this photo. She appeared to be in love with him. His glare was at the camera so I couldn't tell if he felt the same. His posture, his facial expression portrayed an indifferent confidence.

"Who is she?" My words were practically stuck in my throat.

There had been a stranger in my house. Hank tapped his pen to the top of the page. Her name was written: Aria Ritter.

"So, what else did you find out about her?"

"She has three siblings. None of which are Ian. She lives in Philadelphia now, and it seems she has lived in that area her whole life. She did go to Rowan University with Ian, so that was true. And she really is a graphic designer. As far as what makes her tick, why she came into your home, lied to you. That I'm still looking into. Why was she trying to make contact with you? Why did she bring these things to you? Those are still mysteries right now."

"That we are going to solve," Kelly piped up in her evergreen tone.

I couldn't match her enthusiasm. I hated putting this out into the world but I had to ask it. "Was Ian still involved with her?"

Hank shrugged. "Don't have that info yet either, I'm afraid."

I felt a flash of anxiety and just needed to get up and out of the room for a moment. "I need a coffee." I said, standing up. Right now, seemed like a good time to tell them about what I found in the box- and what its significance was. But then I'd have to explain how I got it and I could never do that. I put my hand on the table to stabilize myself as the floor seemed to tilt beneath my feet.

"Are you okay?" Hank asked. I shot him a look that could kill. There was no reason to dignify that with an answer.

The coffee maker was starting to drip and I watched mesmerized. There were times that grief made the world flow in slow motion and all you could do was slow down with it. I filled my cup with the decaf coffee and then added two spoonfuls of sugar. I needed a little extra sweetness right now.

It just hit me that in my haste to get out of the room, I hadn't asked them if they wanted anything. When it was ready, I picked up my mug and headed back to where they were seated to ask if I could get them something. Right before the doorway, I paused when I heard Kelly whispering excitedly to Hank.

I put the mug down and craned my neck so I could hear their hushed tones better.

"This is better than I thought."

"Respectfully—Shut up, Kelly."

"Come on. People are going to eat this shit up. A possible affair?"

"She's in the next room. Could you hide your excitement until you get to the damn car, for Christ's sake? What if she has cameras here and you blow the whole thing?"

She didn't respond and I hung back another moment. "How many times have you scared her off already? You realize you should have been able to record and be done with this podcast in like a week or so of recording."

"She's traumatized," she whispered defensively.

"Yeah, and you clearly don't know how to deal with that."

"What the hell is that supposed to mean?"

"Exactly what I said. If you hadn't been acting a fool, you'd have a podcast done a long time ago."

I heard her huff out a breath with angered exasperation. When I was sure they were done conversing, I re-entered. Kelly was leaning back in the chair, her arms crossed. She looked back at me then she raised her eyebrows.

"Where's your coffee?" she asked, and Hank shot her a look.

Stupidly, I left it on the kitchen countertop while listening to them. I faked a half-hearted laugh. "Whoops! Pregnancy brain." And I walked back to get it. I stole a second in the kitchen trying to think of an excuse to get them out of the house. Right now, I just needed to be alone.

Re-entering with my coffee, I yawned. "I'm sorry to cut this short, but I think I better go back to bed. I'm not feeling well and the pregnancy is making me so tired," I made up on the spot. *Saying I'm about to go to bed with a coffee in my hand—real smooth*. I held up the mug, "Decaf!" I said, with a smile.

They exchanged a quick glance, Hank's facial expression set in stone. The pair got up to leave and wished me well.

Kelly had one foot out the door when she turned around. "Can we meet tomorrow?"

I looked down at the ground and then up at her. "Um, that probably works. Can I text you tonight and let you know how I'm feeling?"

She nodded and locked her eyes on mine. "I'll see you soon." Hank was looking back at her with a stern glare.

I closed the door and pressed my back against the wall as the room spun around me. *What have I gotten myself into?* I thought.

THIRTY-FIVE

The room was icy cold and I pulled the large duvet over my head and snuggled up next to Rosco, hoping to create a bubble of warmth. Stress and anxiety had made it easy to fall asleep but difficult to stay asleep. Sometimes I would take Ian's pillow and pull it towards me, deeply inhaling his fading scent. Sometimes I pushed it to the side, angered that it was a reminder that this used to be a bed for two. "Time heals all. What a God damn lie," I said aloud. Nothing has gotten easier or better as the days went by.

Each day that passed seemed to bring more vivid dreams—as if he was reaching back from the grave into my mind. Begging me not to forget him. Forget us. I had this one dream that came to me so often.

Ian and I are taking the Septa into Philadelphia.

It's strangely empty so I snuggle up to him, draping my legs over his. He places his hand on my thigh, an action he never did in our time together. While I never doubted his love for me, we were never an overly affectionate couple. It's this small element that signals to me that it is just a dream, but as it goes on, my mind blurs the lines. It starts to feel more tangible by the second.

He looks at me like he just fell in love all over again, and I'm soaking it up. This dream is so real, so vivid, that despite the dank smell of the train car, I can physically feel my own happiness. It's like a warmth that radiates off of me.

Then he leans in and the anticipation rises in me. Each millisecond is excruciating. I want to feel him kiss me so badly. Right before his lips are about to touch mine, he evaporates into a black cloud that dissipates. Without his support, I stumble off the seat, trying to claw at the vapor in the air, as if trying to reign it back in, reassemble it so he is back here with me. My outstretched hands curl around the vapors as they slip between my fingers.

"Don't go, stay with me," I cry out. Reaching further, I slip and hit my head on the seat in front of me.

That's when I always wake up, often in a pool of my own sweat.

This night was different, though. I was in the middle of this dream and his lips were hovering close to mine but instead of disappearing like he always does, I felt a physical sensation on my lips, a hand over my mouth.

When it was removed, I called out, "Ian?" And the only response was a cruel laugh. As I turned my head, I saw it was not Ian. There is a stranger in my bed. He reeked of old coffee and motor oil and I recoiled from the smell.

It took me a second to switch from dream to reality. Once the realization sunk in, I was quickly on my feet, grabbing the blanket to cover my body. I scrambled to the corner, legs tangled in the blanket, kicking irrationally to propel me backwards. My heart was racing so fast, I was worried I'd pass out from that alone. I screamed out in pure terror. This is it. Everyone I have ever loved is dead and now I am next.

"Please don't hurt me," I said, knowing it was hopeless. He laughed cruelly again as he sat up in the bed, just watching my panic. I was a caged animal, huddled in the corner, nowhere to go, nothing to defend myself other than a duvet.

Though it was very dark, the numbers on the alarm clock

splice a green light through the room. My eyes adjusted to the minimal light and I could start to see more of his features. A strong jaw, receding hairline, a body rounded in the middle. I couldn't figure out who this was, but I thought I had heard the voice before.

"I'm not here to hurt you."

Fear was now wrapped in confusion. "Why are you here?" If I kept him talking, I could figure out my next step.

"To check in on you, Brittany. I'm never going to hurt you. If I keep you alive, you get to suffer each day knowing the people you love are gone."

Goosebumps prickled my arms as he stood from the bed, watching me for a moment longer. Every muscle in my body was quivering like a plucked guitar string. Heavy steps on the wooden floor were getting closer to me. I tried to push my body closer to the unforgiving wall, trying to climb up it like a terrified rodent.

He brought his face so that it was right beside mine. I could smell the coffee on his breath and it almost made me gag. His lips were just about to touch my ear when he whispered, "It looks like I have another reason to come back." He placed his rough hand on my stomach and every muscle in my body shut down.

"Please stop. Please go away," I cried.

Then, without a word, he got up. I heard his footsteps heavy again but they were growing more distant. Fear pumping through my veins, I didn't move because I still was not convinced that he wouldn't come back to hurt me. I closed my eyes and waited. For hours, I remained locked in place, unsure of what was coming next.

THIRTY-SIX

With my eyes still closed, I felt the soaked sheets beneath me that cooled my skin to the touch. "Shit," I muttered as I realized what had just happened.

I had awoken from the nightmare within a dream, sweat dripping down my forehead, muscles momentarily paralyzed. My whole body felt like it was rattling from within. What could that dream have meant? Dreams and nightmares mean nothing, I tried to tell myself.

There was a large crack of thunder that made me bolt up in bed. Rosco hated storms and went to the window, attempting to scare it away with repeated howls. I turned my head toward the glowing alarm clock. 3:37am. I laid in the bed, listening to the downpour of rain, unable to fully rest. There was no rest, there was no comfort.

After fifteen minutes, I got up and paced the room. My mind flashed to all the people who I didn't trust. Mike, Aria, Kelly and Hank. My mind kept going back to Aria.

Who is Aria Ritter? I flipped over my phone causing the light to sting my eyes. I squinted as I typed her name into Google. I didn't find much that was of use to me. She was awarded the Good Neighbor Award in her town two years ago. She was mentioned as an understudy in a local play a few years before that. So, my Google searches yielded the crucial information that she was a kind-hearted thespian. I tossed the phone onto the nightstand in frustration.

I dragged the box she gave me back into the middle of the living room. Being close to his things brought me a small comfort. His yearbook held memories. His blanket provided him security and warmth. But what about the other thing I found? If she put it there, how did Aria get that and why was she taunting me with it? If someone put it into the box when it was on the porch, when were they coming back and what was their end goal?

The thunder had subsided but the rain was still beating on my windows. Nature's lullaby had calmed both Rosco and myself. He settled on the couch and was fast asleep next to me, lightly snoring.

It occurred to me that I could see if Aria ever appeared in Ian's social media. He was never very active online when we were together. I supposed he had aged out of it. The last post on Instagram was photos from our wedding day. I want to jump back into that moment, reset and start over.

His lack of posting was mismatched with my frequent posting of every trip we took, nice meal we enjoyed and every sunset we watched. We always teased each other about it.

He'd say to me, "Uh oh, time to notify the world we had salad today."

And I'd tease, "Why won't you post a photo of us on IG? Don't want your girlfriend to see?"

Maybe it wasn't a joke after all but a plea for the truth.

My vision was starting to blur from scrolling back so far into his posts. I didn't see a picture of her in any of them, but one comment caught my eye. *What a fun night!* It was a simple message but he didn't reply. The sender: AriaLView-FromTheTop.

I clicked on her profile and went back further and further on her timeline. Unlike my husband, she was a frequent poster, not just in her youth but to this day. It took much longer to get to her college days. There was nothing before that time, then again, social media only came into existence around the time they started college.

She hadn't changed much over the years, seemingly blessed with one of those faces that always leaves you looking a decade younger. Eventually, I spotted him at what appeared to be a college party, and then he was everywhere. She tagged him often, though he never seemed to comment back. It left more questions than answers.

I clicked the little airplane icon and sent it over to Kelly and Hank, pretending that everything was okay. For now, I would ask them for information but I'd be selective on what I'd share until I could figure out if they were trustworthy or not.

Pretty quickly I got a response from Hank.

> You trying to take over my job?

And a few minutes later from Kelly.

> Good work!

I haven't felt proud of anything in so long, it gave me a little spark of happiness. It took so little these days.

> What are you and Hank planning to do next?

> I'm meeting up with Hank tomorrow and we'll figure out the next step. I'll keep you posted.

I quickly gave it a thumbs up and then waited for the sun to rise. Once morning had arrived, I set off, eager to have a long overdue conversation.

Thirty-Seven

Maybe it was the dream, or maybe just the tug of grief, but I felt the need to go visit Ian in his resting place. I grabbed a banana to have as a quick breakfast. The storm from the night before was over, but everything was wet and the high winds hadn't subsided. It wasn't a great day to be outside but I got in the car and headed towards the cemetery, regardless.

The radio was playing bluesy love songs and I couldn't turn it off quick enough. I reached for the dial and swerved a bit into the other lane. Luckily, the roads were mostly empty and I was able to quickly readjust to the correct lane. My hands were shaky and I tried to recall the last time I ate a proper meal. Might have been a full twenty-four hours ago.

I grabbed the browning banana and used my mouth to peel it. The smell was powerful and my throat seemed to heave in and out. If I didn't get away from this smell, I was going to vomit. Without thinking it through, I lowered my window a crack and tossed the whole thing out.

Immediately, red and blue lights flashed in my rear-view mirror and sirens blared.

"Damnit," I muttered, as I pulled the car over.

The officer approached my car and then propped his hand on

the roof as I rolled down my window all the way. A whoosh of air came in. "Ma'am, do you know why I pulled you over?"

"Sorry, I thought it was okay to toss the banana peel on the ground since it is compostable."

He tilted his head, as if he couldn't believe I just said that. "You were driving erratically. Swerving, throwing things onto the road. Hand me your driver's license, registration and insurance, please."

I fumbled in the glove compartment, feeling my anxiety rising. I handed it to him and he looked at the ID for a bit too long, then looked at me long and hard.

"I think I know you..." he said suspiciously.

"Oh really? I don't think we know each other," I responded, trying to play dumb. I lowered my head just a bit, so he could see less of my face.

The officer walked off and I tapped the steering wheel, waiting for him. His red and blue lights still reflecting in the car's mirrors created a chaotic swirl of color. My mind went into overdrive. Had I just given them an opportunity to take me down to the station for questioning?

While I waited for him, I slowly brought air in and out of my lungs, hoping to wash away the anxiety that was making me appear suspicious.

Through the side mirror, I could see him approaching my car. I hoped for a warning but anything short of having to go to the station would be considered a win. In his hand he had a piece of paper that flapped in the wind. I prayed it flew away. The officer passed the ticket through the open window. My eyes scanned for the dollar sign. $250. Damn.

"Where are you heading, Ms. Foster?"

"The cemetery. To visit my husband." He drew in his lips briefly. I had become accustomed to this—the pity, not knowing what to say. So, I filled in the gap. "If everything looks okay, I'd like to be on my way, Officer." My voice as sweet as I could muster it to be in the moment.

"Drive safely. Focus on the road. For your own sake and for those around you. You wouldn't want to be the cause of anyone's death, I'm sure."

I couldn't tell if this was his usual post ticket speech or if he was taking a dig at me. I wasn't hanging around to find out. "Will do," I said and rolled up the window.

Once he was gone, I breathed out, long and slow. I sat there for several minutes, trying to calm my nerves. For a second, I thought of turning back home but continued on my way.

The storm from the night before left the ground soaked and my feet sunk into the muddied pathway with each step. The fierce wind whipped my hair around my face. At points the wind felt so strong that it was practically ushering me towards his gravesite. If I believed in signs, I'd have thought it was a sign of him wrapping his arm around me and bringing me to him.

I pushed the sentimental thought aside. I don't believe in signs. The wind was just a nuisance that was hellbent on messing up my hair.

No matter the time of day, there was always something eerie about walking through a cemetery. People walking around with heads hung low and below our feet are our loved ones, separated by a layer of earth and unfortunate circumstances.

I thought of what I would tell him. And what I would keep to myself for now. I know he can't hear me but there is something healing about having this little plot of land to communicate with him. A place where I can feel that words spoken are received.

Ian's resting place was tucked away towards the back and I rounded the hill. I paused when I saw someone sitting at his grave. This was my first time visiting in a while and yet again I wasn't expecting anyone there. Before I could say anything, she turned around. Upon seeing me, she rose, her knees soaked from the ground.

"Aria?" I asked and she pulled her head back in surprise.

"What are you doing here?" I asked her, my tone more of an accusation than a question.

She tilted her head and took a step back. "How do you know my name?"

"I've found out lots of things. About you and my husband."

"What's that supposed to mean?"

"You lied to me. You aren't related. You didn't grow up together."

She sucked in a breath and her eyes darted to the side. She was clearly trying to figure out how she could escape this uncomfortable situation. But there weren't many places to hide.

I took several steps closer, leaving only a foot between us, trying to make her feel cornered. "I need you to tell me who you are before I call the cops. You entered my home under false pretenses." I had no idea if that was an actual crime but I said it with enough authority that she clearly believed it to be true.

She raised both her hands, like a kid caught stealing from the cookie jar. "Ian and I were college friends. Never anything more."

I searched her face and I was surprised to see disappointment. "Were you close?"

She didn't answer right away and I wasn't sure if she was deciding how to respond or lost in a memory. She bit her lower lip and then said, "We were."

"You loved him, didn't you?"

She raised her eyebrows. "I don't know. I mean, I guess it could be called that."

"And he didn't reciprocate?"

Aria shrugged her shoulders. "Always the friend, never anything more."

I nodded. "So how did you really come to have his things and end up at my doorstep?"

"He contacted me a while ago. He gave me an address, a key and a number. Said if anything happened, to go to the storage unit, get the contents and give it all to you. That's all."

"What about Mike? Was any of that true?"

"Yeah, I met him through Ian, while making the logo for Gritty Grinds. We went out once," she looked off to the side and smiled. "I guess I was trying to see if I could make Ian jealous. Didn't work." She raised her eyebrows and rolled her eyes. "He was the one who called to tell me Ian had passed. Then he was like, Maybe we could get a drink after the funeral."

My face contorted. "What a creep," I said.

"Yup. But he didn't tell me about the storage. That was all Ian. But it's good you have it right?"

I didn't reply, lost in thought. Why would my husband, so young and healthy, be worried about something happening? Why would he give it to some casual acquaintance?

Then it all made sense. Ian knew what was going to happen to him. He was the last person I loved. Despite all his claims that these things were a terrible coincidence, in the back of his mind, he must have been waiting for his turn.

And he loved me anyway.

I'm like a disease, reaching out to infect and harm those around me. Thinking of the mental anguish he must have been in that last year, the months leading up to that final March 13th must have been excruciating and he suffered alone, trying to keep me calm.

My knees felt weak and then I collapsed to the ground. My husband lived with the fear that something would happen to him, because he was with me. He loved me enough to stay, and it killed him.

Aria knelt down and her hand was on my back as I began to sob. The grief, the guilt, the injustice. It was all too much. Her touch was a small comfort at first but then I pulled away. I did not know who this woman was. I didn't know her motives.

When the tears stopped, I looked up at her.

"Are you going to be okay here? I can stay nearby if you'd like," she asked, her eyes searching mine with genuine concern.

"No, thank you," I responded. There was a long silence and I wasn't sure what to say.

"It's okay," she said standing back up. "I understand. I'll go, so you can have some time alone together."

All the things I planned to say to Ian had vanished from my thoughts. I knelt at the front of the headstone, not caring that the ground was damp and soaking through my jeans. My hand instinctively reached for the cold stone, mentally replacing this slab of stone for him. It's all I had left. This headstone and a box of mysteries.

"I miss you," I said, the words hanging in the air, never to be reciprocated.

"And I'm so sorry but thank you for loving me until the very end."

Since running into Aria earlier that day, it was all I could think about. I needed to know more about her.

> Any luck?

I texted Hank.

While I waited for an answer, I opened up Ian's Facebook again, searching for more connections between him and Aria.

He responded several minutes later.

> Still working on it.

I tried to stifle my frustration. I needed answers now.

My thumb swiped up over and over, trying to get back to the photo I found originally. Her gaze at him was loving but maybe also a bit disturbing. It showed so much longing. She claimed he never reciprocated and even though he's gone, she was still hanging on to this obsession. Why else would she bother getting his things and then make the effort to deliver them to me?

Thirty-Eight

Since the baby was due soon, less than two months, I messaged Kelly for an update on the podcast. We had started this project months ago and it was taking entirely too long. I really wanted answers before the baby came. And with only one-hundred and sixty days until the next March 13th, I was growing desperate.

We hadn't recorded in a long time and I was thankful for the distance. Her first vision was to have this whole podcast mostly be a dialogue between the two of us but over time it evolved. She had attended several workshops about podcasting and a few true crime conventions. So, it became something much more complicated, much more well designed...or that was at least what she had communicated to me. I had no actual proof that's what was happening.

She planned to add in news clips, additional interviews with people who were affected by each individual death as well as law enforcement. Overall, I was just happy that it lightened how much I needed to participate. I could soon put this all behind me.

So, when she messaged me:

Could we do another recording session?

I was surprised. Looking at the screen for a long time, I rested my hand on my large belly. "What do I do? What do I do?" I said aloud. I wasn't eager to see her again, but it was now or never.

Sure, when is a good time?

With the last conversation I overheard between her and Hank in my mind, I walked into Kelly's studio with apprehension. I kept telling myself it would be okay but just to stay alert. She was in this for the wrong reasons but harmless. Right?

A wave of panic washed over me as Kelly hit record on the device, oversized microphones set up before each of us. The walls were now lined with thick gray acoustic foam. No one would hear me if I screamed. *Shit. Why the hell did I agree to come here?* asked the voice in my head.

"We have to go over something we already recorded. I had to scrap it because there was so much background noise," she said, and she gestured toward the foam walls. "Like the upgrade?"

I nodded.

"Ready?" But she'd already hit record. What choice did I have? "Today we're talking about the third loss." Her voice and cadence were different now, as if she flipped a switch and became a presenter or a newscaster. This hadn't been the case in our previous sessions, where she was more casual, more informal. I wondered if attending all those true crime conferences went to her head a bit.

"Amanda," I said softly. She put out her hand and lifted it up, signaling me to speak louder. "My friend, Amanda, passed away, after my best friend, and my..." It became difficult to speak, like my mind and mouth filled with concrete at the same time.

"Your parents," Kelly said, assisting me.

I nodded. She started to move her hands in small circles, trying to encourage me to say more on the topic. We hadn't met in so long, and so much had changed, I was starting to feel like I just couldn't do this. But her eyes on me made me spit something out.

"We were part of a trio. We rode our bikes everywhere, as far as you can go at that age. Our families even once did a group vacation to LBI when we were in first grade."

"Tell us a little bit more about her. What was Amanda like?"

Some pictures of her flashed through my mind. Mini moments that have stuck with me all these years later. But most of it was hazy. It was so long ago, and we fell out of contact after I moved.

"From what I remember, we were all very close that first year. We were all in the same class together. We were in different classes in 2nd grade but remained close, still seeing each other during lunch and recess. But something happened after that trip to the beach. Amanda wasn't allowed to hang out with us as much. I guess as a kid, I just thought she was busy or her parents were really strict."

"Is that how you still see it today?"

"Yes," I told her, though I knew it wasn't true. I knew something no one else knew. It wasn't relevant so there was no sense in bringing up old secrets and exposing past wrongs.

"You said trio. Why don't you tell us a little bit about who else was in that trio?"

My eyes went wide. This wasn't part of the plan—at least not yet. I looked at her shaking my head. I won't talk about this. When we started this project, we had agreed to really focus on those five years and not focus on past drama.

She tossed up her hands in defeat but seemed to quickly regain herself. Kelly melted back into her newscaster voice. "There are some who speculate that Amanda's death wasn't really part of this equation since you weren't all that close at this point in your life. What are your thoughts on that?"

"I think they are all connected. The connection is me. Either there is some dark force around me or someone is trying to hurt me."

"But why?" she asked while looking at her laptop.

I waited for her to meet my gaze, stern and cold, and mouthed silently, "You know why."

August 1998

Long Beach Island, NJ Beach rental

Waves and laughter filled the air as seagulls soared above us. We were so young, just eight-years-old, so summer stretched into eternity like the ocean before us.

It was our last night at the beach house. Amanda's parents, my parents and Anna's parents were all inside, probably enjoying a 'grown up' drink as they called them. We had been playing tag and I was running with all my might. Anna was chasing me and I tripped, falling face first into the sand.

"Pfft!" I said, standing up and spitting out the hoarse granules stuck to my tongue. "Where's Amanda?" I asked, and then spat again, still feeling the gritty pieces in my mouth.

Anna looked around. "Uh oh!"

Holding hands, we ran back towards the house, the ocean breeze at our backs.

Not seeing her right away, Anna took charge, like she normally did. "You look in the back and I'll look in the front of the house." And as I normally did, I obeyed.

We divided, trying to find our friend. The grownups were very strict about us staying together, and we didn't want to get in trouble on our last night and risk losing ice cream as a punishment. I heard something almost immediately from under the deck. It sounded like sniffling.

"Amanda?" I whispered.

She didn't respond, but I crawled under, feeling broken shells poking into my palms and knees, enveloped in darkness.

"Where are you? I can't see you," I called out as a cobweb covered my face. "Ugh, gross," I said, wiping off the strands.

She still didn't answer, but I followed the sound of her sniffles.

I sat next to my friend and asked her what was wrong. She continued to cry but did not answer me. Clearly, she didn't want to talk. I tried to put my arm around her but she shrugged it off. "Come on, let's go back in."

"No!" she shouted, breaking her silence.

"Okay, okay," I tried to soothe. I had no clue what was wrong, so I wasn't sure what to say or do. So, I just sat there with her, raking my hands through the damp sand in search of a shell to play with.

I had what felt like six broken shells in my hand when she finally spoke. "I'm never going back in there."

"What happened, Amanda? We were all having fun."

She started sobbing loudly. "Anna's dad!" she said. "He's an asshole!"

I remember recoiling at her words. I hadn't heard a kid talk like that ever—and about a grown up!

"I ran inside to get my sweater. I was in my mom's closet when they came into my parents' bedroom. I froze. He said he needed to talk to my mom about how sick his wife was. He said he needed a friend. She said she was there for him. I didn't hear him say anything back, but then I heard her scream out. She said, 'stop touching me'. He called her a bad name, Brittany. A very bad name! He left, slamming the door behind him. I was stuck in the closet while I heard her crying. I didn't know what to do."

"Oh my god. I'm sorry. He shouldn't have said a bad word."

"Brittany! He hurt her!"

"Oh." I didn't fully understand. Not at that moment.

That was the last time I hung out with Amanda. She and her family left the beach house early the next morning, before anyone else had even woken up. There was no goodbye. She was forbidden to hang out with us after that. I'd see her at school, passing in the hall-ways, and she always looked away.

Back then, I wasn't sure why she wouldn't talk to me. I hadn't done anything wrong.

But now, as an adult, with the memories slowly returning, I understand so much more.

Once we returned from the beach house, there was just one week left of summer. And that last week, I should have been focused on my return to school, about starting 3ʳᵈ grade, but all I could think about was what Amanda had told me.

"Mom?"

"Yeah," she said, keeping her eyes focused on the TV. She was watching The Jerry Springer Show and didn't bother to turn it down or off as the screen displayed three adults breaking into a violent fight.

"Did Anna's dad ever hurt you?"

That got her eyes off the TV. She muted the show and turned towards me. She said nothing at first but scanned my face, as if she was looking for clues. Finally, she spoke. "No, of course not. He's a nice man." She bit her lower lip.

"Well, did he ever," I paused, afraid to ask, afraid of her reaction. "Did he ever touch you?"

"Jesus Christ, Brittany! What a question to ask!" She nearly bounced out of the recliner and took my chin in her hand, gripping it too hard. It hurt, but I was too scared to tell her that. "I don't want you to ask stupid questions like that ever again. Such a stupid, stupid question. Never again! Do you understand me?" she ranted as her face grew red as a Jersey tomato.

I tried to nod but her hold on my chin was so firm that it couldn't move. "Yes," I squeaked out so she would let me go. When she released her hand, I could still feel it there.

"Stupid questions are asked by stupid girls. You aren't a stupid girl, are you?"

My head shook from side to side, too afraid to speak. I wanted to get out of the living room so I could break down, because I didn't want to let her see me cry.

When she reached for the remote and turned the volume back up, I ran to my room, slamming the door behind me. I tossed myself onto my bed and cried for what felt like the whole night. My mother did not come in to comfort me. When my father came home from work, she greeted him warmly as if nothing was wrong.

"Where's my girl?" I heard him ask.

"I'm right here," she said, attempting to flirt, and it made me feel icky.

"I'm asking where Brittany is."

I heard her puff out air. "Just in her room being anti-social as usual," she told him, as if she wasn't the reason I was in there.

"Don't call her that. She's allowed to have her own space away from the chaos."

That pissed her off and they started to argue. "What chaos? Tell me! I do everything for you, so what actual problems could you have, Lenard?" I heard her slam down a glass.

"You don't give me any peace."

I put the pillow over my head to drown it out, but it became hard to breathe.

Wiping away my tears, I went out in the hallway and saw them standing near the entryway. They turned towards me. I felt so bad for my dad but didn't run to him, worried it would set her off.

Luckily, he came to me and gave me a hug. He said, "Let's watch some TV."

Without a word, I followed him into the living room. I prayed she wouldn't join us but she did. I crawled into his lap, and he turned on Full House.

"Woah! You haven't done this since you were little. Everything okay?" he said as he wrapped his arms around me.

"She's fine. She's fine!" my mother said, her voice firm, as her leg bobbed up and down rapidly. She left the living room and when she

returned, she placed a wooden tray in front of us. Then she threw down two lukewarm TV dinners. Her lips were so tight that they nearly disappeared. The whole time she was keeping her eyes on me as I nuzzled closer to him.

Thirty-Nine

The sheet from Dr. Katz listed the many things to do during pregnancy, and I had been following them closely since the day she handed me this paper. Fresh air and exercise were high on the list, so I leashed up Rosco and set out for a long walk with him. I was walking much slower these days, but he didn't seem to mind. After he and I had made the rounds of the neighborhood, I told him it was time to head back home. I was exhausted, both mentally and physically. Today would have been our wedding anniversary. I thought about how we might have celebrated today, knowing we had a baby due any day now. Maybe we would have gone to the coffee shop where we had our first date, to marvel at how much had changed since that day.

I tried to picture our first date, but the image of him isn't as vivid as it used to be. There were two mugs of coffee, a berry scone and a chocolate chip muffin. I wore a new purple top, or was it red? I can't recall. It doesn't matter either way. What I do remember, what I'll never forget, is the way he smiled at me throughout the night and how it made me feel. The embers of our relationship are there but they are flickering.

As I rounded the corner, I spotted something on my porch.

It's a bouquet of white roses. I let Rosco in and stayed outside with the flowers, looking at them uncertainly. There was a small card, and I reached down and grabbed it with unsteady hands as Rosco's face peered through the window as if asking, "Why didn't you come in too?"

I pulled the card from the red envelope. It read:

You were always the one.

The card fell from my hands, and I looked around frantically, as if the sender would be lurking nearby.

My next-door neighbor, an elderly woman came out, not noticing my panic. "Oh, good! You got them. What's the occasion?"

Good lord, there was no explaining this quickly. "Uh, hi Betty. These must have been delivered to the wrong address, actually. Did you see who dropped it off?"

"There was a white van parked in front of your house a bit ago. I think it was Beautiful Bouquets...Or Bountiful Bouquets. Something like that. They actually came to my door first. Looking for a Brittany. That's you, right dear?"

Despite the fact that the doors to our condos were feet away from each other, I hadn't spoken to her much.

I nodded.

"Okay, good, because I told them I believed you lived here. Glad it got to the right house! Though I wouldn't have minded some flowers," she said laughing at her own joke.

I forced the corners of my lips up in an attempt to smile back. Leave it to the retired neighbor to have the details. I muttered a quick thanks, leaving the flowers outside and dashed into the house.

Once I located the shop's phone number, I called in. "Hi, my name is Brittany. I just received a bouquet of flowers at my house." I faked a small chuckle. "Seems the sender forgot to sign their name and I was wondering if you could look it up so I know who to send a thank you message to."

I heard some light typing on the other end. "Yes, oh yes! I actually remember this because it was such a touching story. They are from Ian Foster."

I looked at the card again. You were always the one. I shook my head. The message was sweet but strange. It's vague. It's unsigned. It had beautiful flourishes and was far too elaborate to be his handwriting. It looked like a woman's writing.

"That can't be right. My husband passed seven months ago."

I heard her gasp. "Oh dear. I'm so sorry to hear that. He seemed like such a resourceful guy." I furrowed my brow.

"What do you mean?"

"He told me he traveled a lot for work and wanted to make sure you got your anniversary flowers so he prepaid for the ones you got today. I'd never had anyone ask for that before, but I thought it was very sweet. Clearly, he loved you a lot. He told me the message, and I filled out the card. He asked me to include it with your flowers, so I've had it in my desk drawer for a year now. I normally don't do that...but, well, he paid me a bit extra and..." her voice trailed off.

"It's fine. Was that it? Like, did he only pay for this one year or were there others?"

"Just this one. Honestly, probably couldn't have kept track of it beyond that, anyway." She laughed to herself.

"Thank you," I said and quickly hung up.

He had never done anything like that in the past. I didn't even get flowers for our last anniversary, so he walked into this flower shop and prepaid for flowers but didn't pick any up for the current anniversary? It made no sense.

It also was just so out of character for him. In fact, he completely forgot about our second dating anniversary and when he picked me up, I was all dolled up and he was in gym clothes. I'd stormed back inside, and he texted me from the car.

Don't be mad. I'll make it up to you.

But I wasn't angry. When I'd come back outside, I was in gym clothes too. "McDonalds or Wendys?" I'd asked him.

It became a running joke between us. Pre-planning an anniversary a year in advance just didn't seem like something he would do.

FORTY

Eyeing the flowers suspiciously, an overwhelming chill sank into my skin and a small voice whispered, 'Get the hell out of here.' The sun was shining though autumn was upon us and it was starting to feel cool outside. I hopped into the car and put Haddonfield into my GPS with the plan of just walking along the street, window shopping. A sense of dread was creeping up, but I told myself it would be all right, that I needed the exercise and to get out of the house.

I parked near the large dinosaur statue that boasted about Haddonfield being the site of the first ever fully found dinosaur skeleton. It brought a smile to my face because I could picture pushing a stroller down these sidewalks one day and showing my toddler this statue.

A nice fall breeze fluttered vibrant leaves around me, but few people were out. Along the sidewalk, I went out of my way to stomp on the large crunchy leaves, a habit I picked up in childhood and never kicked. My nerves started to settle a bit, and I glanced in windows looking at things I definitely didn't need. One store had the cutest sports hoodies in deep green with white writing for the favorite local football team. It was like a religion here. I thought about going in but realized I couldn't fit into that for a while, anyway.

In the next window, I saw calendars for the next year. 2026 was upon us—a year in which Ian will have never existed. My chest tightened. I wanted to linger in this year where I still had my husband a little longer. The chiming of the bell at midnight would be lonely, without our usual kiss and then it would usher in a full year without him. Holidays will come, and they will be my first time celebrating them as a widow. I shook my head, feeling too overwhelmed and continued to wander.

I made my way down the street and was peering into a small bookshop, looking at a display of kids books that I could imagine reading at bedtime. How much was in my bank account? I wondered and started to do the mental calculations to see if I could afford a few of the books. I was coming to the realization that it's either buying these books or being able to cover all my monthly bills when I heard my name. It was harsh like sandpaper. Before I could turn around, they'd grabbed my wrist to spin me in their direction. My body froze up at the unexpected aggression.

"What the hell are you up to?" Mike barked at me.

I was still frozen in fear but needed to get my hand away from him. I began to pull my arm back and he let go. "How did you know where I'd be?" I asked, my voice soft, both to try to calm him and to not bring attention to us.

"Know you'd be here? I'm setting up a Gritty Grinds down the street."

"You didn't tell me."

He shook his head. "I don't have to tell you. And I sure as shit won't be sharing things with you now that I know what you're pulling. I paid you for six months out of generosity. You realize I didn't have to do that, right? And this is how you repay me?"

A bell chimed as a customer walked out of the bookshop and Mike softens his facial features, letting the rage be less visible, but I was sure it was still boiling inside him. The customer, with two books in hand, eyed us but either didn't notice my distress or didn't care.

"I'm not sure what you're talking about." I hoped my voice didn't betray me and let him know how terrified I was.

"The fucking will, Brittany. You sent a lawyer after me! Do you know how much this is going to cost me? And for what? Ian and I were together when it was drafted. I told you that. Now I have to pay my lawyer to talk to your lawyer about something you already know. It's bullshit. Expensive bullshit. I knew I shouldn't have paid you anything."

I stepped back from him because I was unsure if he was going to put his hands on me again. At this point, I just needed to focus on self-preservation.

"I'll contact my lawyer and tell him to drop it," I said.

"Do it now. In front of me." The rage he hid from that passing customer was back on full display.

I was shocked at how his aggression was escalating right there in public. With trembling hands, I reached into my back pocket for my phone. Before I could even finish typing in my passcode, we turned towards the bell chime. The bookshop door opened again.

We both looked at the lanky man standing in the doorway as he peered at us, trying to assess the situation. He wore a tan button-down cardigan that made him appear like a younger Mr. Rogers. He asked calmly, "Is everything okay?"

I looked at him, my eyes pleading for help but my mouth staying silent. Thankfully, he recognized my desperation.

"Why don't you come inside ma'am?" He ushered me over to a wooden bench and all the emotion I had been holding in came to the surface. I was crying into my hands when I heard him say, "Should I call the police?"

I shook my head no. "Is that man gone?"

The front of the store was all windows and he looked from side to side. "It looks like it."

I didn't watch Mike leave, so I don't know which way he

went. Maybe he was waiting for me somewhere just out of sight. If he could be that aggressive with people around, what would he do if we were alone?

"Can someone walk me to my car, please? I'm just parked over there," I said pointing down the street.

"Sure. Let me just tell my co-worker that I'm stepping out for a minute."

We walked in silence the short distance. When we got to my car, I turned to thank him. "Will you be okay? Do you feel okay to drive? Because you're welcome to come back into the store and stay longer if you need to. There is no rush, really."

"No, I think I just need to get home. Thank you though. I appreciate your kindness." He gave me a small smile and his eyes lingered on me for a moment.

As soon as I closed the car door, I pulled away, driving a few miles above the speed limit, eager to leave this situation behind me. Sitting at a red light, it hit me later that Mike didn't seem surprised to see me eight months pregnant. Who had told him?

FORTY-ONE

few days ago, I reached out to Aria on Facebook, asking her to meet up. We agreed to grab breakfast together at a diner on route 70. I swear this area gets more congested each time I go out so of course traffic had me running late. When I walked in, the smell of coffee and so many different foods overwhelmed me, causing a lump in my throat. I looked around then I spotted her, already seated.

She was wearing an oversized black shirt, as if she was trying to hide herself. I slid into the booth across from her, unsure if I would be able to eat.

"Sorry I'm late."

"No problem. You look great! You are glowing. When's the baby due?"

"About four weeks!" I said. "Thanks for meeting with me. I have a few questions that I need to clear up."

Aria closed her eyes briefly and nodded.

The waitress came up to our table and pulled out a small notepad. "What can I get you today?"

"Just a decaf coffee for me...actually a pork roll sandwich too...and hash browns. A side of fruit too, please," I said.

"Anything else?" she said sarcastically as she scribbled my order onto her notepad.

"A side of pickles," I added a bit embarrassed, looking at my hands, imagining her rolling her eyes at me.

"Anything else?" she repeated.

I shook my head and she turned to Aria. "I'll have the same- minus the pickles."

"Kay," the waitress said flatly.

Once she left, I jumped right into the conversation, propping my elbows on the table and leaning into her.

"So, you didn't grow up with Ian?"

"No, I lied about that. I thought you'd be more likely to let me in and talk with me if I was part of his family and not just some random stranger dropping off a box. Sorry. We met at Rowan. On the first day in fact. He was living on my dorm floor, and I bumped into him. Spilled my coffee everywhere. He joked that it was a good thing I did that because it was a shitty coffee anyway. He hated the big coffee chains. A coffee guy even back then. He invited me into his room for coffee, and I thought he was hitting on me! But no, he made me a pour-over coffee with beans he got from Ethiopia," she said, shaking her head at the memory. "After college, we kept in touch. Ya know, through Facebook mostly. I'd always call him up and invite him out, but we rarely met up after his shop really took off. I miss him. It's been—"

"Seven months," I finished her sentence and she looked beyond me while nodding. "What was he like back then?"

The waitress put down the two coffees. "Creamer and sugar over there," she said, pointing to two small ceramic bowls.

Aria added two sugars to her mug while she smiled. I could tell she was remembering fond moments. I was trying to be patient with her but I needed her to get on with it. She told me a few anecdotes before our food arrived, piping hot. I used my fork to move around the hash browns, playing with my food like a little kid. I was too interested in what she was about to say to eat.

"He was always a good friend. He was always very sensitive for a guy, especially back then. But I suppose that came about from what he experienced." She picked at the fruit, trying to see her options before selecting a slice of pineapple and taking a bite.

I was not sure what she was talking about. "Experienced? What do you mean?" I asked, raising my eyebrows, eager to hear what she was about to say.

"The family tragedy," she stated solemnly, as if I should know what she's talking about.

She noticed the blank look on my face and her eyes seemed to be searching my expression for understanding. "How his sister died. And then his mom. And his father was so distraught that he took his own life. Ian had to go live with his grandmother. Sadly, she also passed away. I think when he was eighteen, maybe nineteen. He was all alone at that point."

I'd stopped playing with my food, fully focused on what she was saying.

"He was always scarred by what happened as a kid, but losing his grandma was like the last straw. He couldn't handle the fact that he was all alone, having to go the rest of his life without any family. It all made him so despondent. But even with that, I loved him so much. Maybe I thought I could help him," she said shaking her head again as she stirred her coffee. She sighed and then continued, "I tried to connect with him but the more I tried, the more he pulled away."

Our coffees and breakfast platters sat on the table untouched and growing cold.

I froze, knowing what I needed to ask next but not wanting to. "What happened to his sister? How did she die?" My heart was beating with such fervor that it seemed like it was trying to escape my body.

She furrowed her brow, like she was suspicious of me now. "I know he didn't really like talking about it much. But you were his wife. He didn't tell you any of this?" She took the ketchup bottle and slathered her sandwich in it and then took a bite. The red liquid oozed out the sides, splattering on the plate.

A scowl was my only response so she continued. "She died in a biking accident. When she was in 2nd or 3rd grade. It was really tragic. He said he was never the same after that. More withdrawn. Quick to anger as a kid. When I first met him, he was sometimes quick to fly off the handle, sometimes wouldn't respond for days. But he changed that last year of college. It was more like a low-level simmer. I assumed it was because he got therapy and didn't tell me, or was self-medicating. Once he calmed down, he always seemed to be somewhere else though."

My heart was racing so fast and I put my hand over my chest. But I couldn't leave until she confirmed what I felt like I already knew. "What was his sister's name?"

She tilted her head. "You don't know his sister's name?"

"God damn it!" I slammed my fist on the table and the plates and cutlery jumped in surprise. A waitress walking by stopped and looked our way, assessing if this was going to escalate or not. I ignored her. "What was his sister's name?" My voice was more like a growl.

She was taken aback but answered me anyway.

"Anna. Her name was Anna." She lowered her head as my whole body revolted. I leaned over the edge of the booth and vomited all over the floor.

December 1998

Blackwood, NJ

When the bell rang at the end of the day, we packed up our things and I said to Anna, "I'll see you tomorrow." Her dad always picked her up in a sporty blue convertible.

"Hey, wait," she called.

I pretended I couldn't hear her because I was eager to get away. I didn't ever want to see her awful dad again.

"My dad said he can't get me today, so he dropped me off this morning with my bike."

"Why?"

"Why what?"

"Why can't he get you, Anna? What's he doing?"

She wrinkled her face like a pug and for the first time I thought she looked ugly. "I don't know! But I can ride home with you! He gave me $5. We can get candy at Wawa."

I looked away. "I don't have any money," I said.

She playfully pushed my shoulder and I held myself back from pushing her to the ground. "I said I have five bucks! I can get you candy too."

"Thanks," I muttered, wishing I had my own money, not her money, not her cheating daddy's money.

We started to pedal away from school. She was in the lead, because she never let me go first. She was chatting away to me and all I could think was how clueless she was. "So, I said to my dad, if I don't get that Furby, I'll be the only kid in school without one."

I can't hear her. The traffic is busy even though it is too early for grownups to be driving home from work. "What!" I call up to her as a large truck passes by. The loud engine sound is deafening. She shouts it again but louder. "But that's not even true!" I shout back. This time it's her turn to not hear.

Something about the buzz of the traffic, knowing she won't hear me.

Something about the independence and freedom of riding your bike with the wind in your hair.

Something about it makes me want to do something crazy and stupid.

I decide to make a confession.

"Your dad is kissing my mom," I shout, but at the moment I do, there's a small clearing in the traffic and she hears me.

Her bike screeches to a halt and I nearly crash into her. "What did you just say?"

"Nothing." All my fearlessness flew away, and I'm terrified.

"You are a liar! A stupid, ugly, liar."

"No! Your dad's a bad man. He tried to kiss Amanda's mom too. Ask her! Why do you think she can't talk to us anymore? Because your dad's a jerk!"

She gasps. "My dad wouldn't like your mother. She's not even half as pretty as my mom."

"Your dad hates her! That's why he tries to kiss everyone else!" I shot back.

She shrieked. "I hate you!" she yelled, tears wetting her cheeks. "I'm going home and telling my mom and dad what you just said, then you're going to be in big trouble."

She starts to pedal away and I follow her in a panic. I can't have this get out—it will kill my dad. My mom will probably keep me locked in the closet and never speak to me again. Or maybe her dad and my mom will end up living together, and she will make me live with that gross man. The panic is rising and it is making me erratic. My brain is being controlled by my emotions, and every-thing else is blocked out.

I pedal up to the left side of her, practically edging her off the sidewalk.

"Stop! There isn't room," she yells at me.

I don't respond. I extend my hand and just push. She wobbled, screamed and then my memory goes blank.

Forty-Two

The memory assaulted me, as if I were reliving it. My appetite vanished and I quickly asked for the check. "I have to go," I said to Aria.

She wrinkled her brow causing little hills to form on her forehead but I didn't acknowledge her confusion. I threw down a fifty-dollar bill before it even arrived and scooted out from the booth. I bolted up from my seat.

"What's wrong?" she asked.

I mumbled a quick goodbye. I was unable to bear this news and all that it meant. I left the food, not even bothering to have it boxed up. Food was the farthest thing from my mind at that point. My fight or flight had kicked into high drive, and it chose flight. Once I was outside, I felt as if I was running through our whole lives together at warp speed. Each moment, each memory, now seen from a different angle.

As I was seeing these things through a new lens, each of the puzzle pieces started to fit into place. But I didn't have all the answers. Who was my husband? Why did this connection bring us together? And who took him away from me?

Inside our home, I dashed to our room and rummaged through the nightstand for his phone. I plugged it in and waited impatiently for it to power up. The few seconds stretched on and on and I shook the phone as if it would help speed up the process. Finally, it illuminated and asked for his password. I typed in the date of Anna's death. Nothing. I tried to recall her birthday but nothing came to mind. I racked my brain for any other connections. Then, I googled the obituary for Anna and Ian's father. My eyes searched rapidly, desperate for information. At the bottom paragraph was the information for his funeral. March 13th, 1999.

I typed in 03-13-99. The phone unlocked. All the apps had been deleted and all I could see was the Home Screen wallpaper. It had always been our wedding photo, but it was replaced with a message.

Hello, Brittany.

I looked up, gazing at the wall but seeing our whole life in front of us. This man. This man that I loved with every ounce of my being. This man, whose absence this past year had torn away the only thing in my life that had ever felt right. Who the hell was he?

FORTY-THREE

For two weeks, my every thought I had was focused on to figure out who the hell I had married. I wasn't eating. I wasn't sleeping. I kept composing messages to Kelly and Hank, thinking they could get me answers...but every time I'd remind myself that they'd learn more about what happened to Anna and so I'd hit delete.

So, when my stomach clenched, I chalked it up to stomach pains caused by the overwhelming amount of stress. When it happened a third time, I wonder if I could possibly be going into labor though it was still two weeks until my due date. As I was about to call my OB/GYN, a flash of liquid went down my legs. It was time. I opened my phone and ordered a Lyft.

When the driver arrived, I placed one hand on the car and one hand on my stomach. I huffed out, "I'm in labor. Can you—" and then I stopped talking and closed my eyes, mentally trying to get through this contraction. The poor young man's eyes widened. He certainly wasn't expecting this today.

"Okay, lady. Get in."

I struggled to get into the back seat and once I did, I apologized over and over through the contractions.

He pulled up to the front of the hospital. "Let me help you in."

"You really don't need...ahhhh!" And he took my arm and helped me walk in.

"She needs a wheelchair. She's in labor," he called out into the lobby.

"Okay dad, we got it," said the young woman in pink scrubs to the man fifteen years my junior. We both turned to each other and laughed...and then I balled my fists and screamed again from a pain greater than anything I had ever experienced.

The driver put his hand on my shoulder, said, "Good luck!" And walked out the door.

"Here you go," said the nurse returning with the wheelchair. "Husband's off to park the car?"

"Yeah," I said, because that was a lot less depressing than explaining I was going to be going into labor completely alone.

Nearly twenty-four hours later, I was on the brink of exhaustion when the midwife said, "Just one more push."

Hearing that, I was able to muster some energy and a minute later, I heard the cries of my baby.

"It's a girl!" she exclaimed.

They took the baby to be cleaned, and minutes later she was laying on my chest with a pink and blue blanket rested on top of her.

We laid there, providing each other warmth, and I had never felt more connected to another human in my life. "Please never leave me," I repeated with each rise and fall of her little chest. My lips met the top of her head and I kissed her gently. I was no longer alone.

FORTY-FOUR
THURSDAY, MARCH 13, 2025

My daughter, Mable, lay in my arms, her warm soft skin flush against mine as she nursed. The navy-blue rocking chair swayed back and forth to calm both of us. Her milky scent brought comfort even on the long sleepless nights. The past four and a half months with her had been the greatest of my life. I watched as her little chest went up and down, fixated on this marvel of life.

I whispered to her, "Today is for us."

We would take this day back, not as a day to focus on all the grief but to focus on each other, to be thankful we are alive. I didn't have all the answers, but starting the day, something told me that the harrowing chapter of my life was over. I could now focus on raising my daughter and healing my open wounds.

When she unlatched, I pulled down my nightshirt and stood with her, swaying side to side. She drifted off to sleep in my arms and I tip-toed toward the curtains, pulling it back just a sliver so I could look outside.

The sun was rising, but there were thick gray clouds plastering the sky. I could barely see glimmers of light through the small openings. *This isn't good,* I thought to myself, quickly abandoning my positivity from moments earlier. I'd rarely tried to catch meaning in the things around me. They often end up being wrong but still I felt like this was a sign. A bad sign.

I woke up on this day to celebrate with a sunrise, and it was shrouded in darkness. *This means something* I repeated over and over in my head. I put Mable down into her bassinet, afraid a panic attack might strike. She must be kept safe, especially today.

The transfer from my arms to her soft white bassinet made her stir momentarily, but then she fell back to sleep. Deep inhales and exhales, I told myself to try to ward off the rush of fear. What can I do to protect her? I grabbed my phone from the charger, but I can't call the police and tell them I need help.

"Hello, officer. I'm afraid of March 13th. Can you please send someone to watch over me for twenty-four hours?" I'd get committed for a call like that.

Then, my phone buzzed with a familiar number.

"Hank? What—," I started, but he cut me off.

"I have something I need to show you."

"What is it?" My voice was shaky like the tremble from an earthquake.

"It's better to tell you in person."

"Just tell me!" I shouted, and it caused both Mable and Rosco to awaken but I realized he had already hung up. I patted Rosco while gently rocking the bassinet back and forth. Both were calmed in minutes while I was left with my brain rapidly firing off all the possible scenarios of what he could need to tell me. Was someone hurt? But who could that possibly be? There's no one left except my daughter, my dog and me and we are all safe in this room. For now.

I placed my pinkie near her hand, and even through sleep she instinctively wrapped her little fingers around it. Though I'm the mother, I let her provide me with comfort until Hank arrived with whatever news he had. As I waited, I couldn't take my eyes off her, watching her small movements as she slept, a confirmation that she was okay.

FORTY-FIVE

Hank was at my door within fifteen minutes, and I turned on the baby monitor. I looked through the peep hole to see him standing there with a black laptop bag slung over his shoulder. I was trying to remain calm as I opened the door. "Who died?" I said immediately.

He started to shake his head and then his face softened. "Oh my God, I'm so sorry. It's not like that."

I motioned for him to come in. "So, everything's okay?" I asked, releasing the tension from each of my muscles like the waves rescinding during low tide. With the baby monitor in my hand, I kept looking down at the screen to see both Mable and Rosco were still asleep.

Hank paused, as if he was unsure what to say.

"Everyone's okay right now. Let's sit down," he said, using his hands as he spoke to pacify me.

"Just so you know, I have cameras all around the house."

"Um, okay. Cool. That's probably a good idea," he said.

Though he was still dressed in his black rock band shirt, his cool-guy attitude was gone. He was much calmer than the last time he'd spoken to me. This change in demeanor was having the opposite effect as it was putting me on edge.

"Tell me why you are here. Whatever it is," I implored.

"Okay, but please take some deep breaths while I get it ready," he said as he pulled his device out of the black bag. His request only heightened my anxiety and I tried to run through the list of people I still knew that could be in harms way while staring down at the baby monitor. *She's safe,* I kept repeating in my head.

"Hank, where's Kelly? Is she okay?" I asked.

"Hmmm mmm," he said, placing the laptop on the coffee table.

My eyes were darting back and forth between the monitor and Hank.

With his laptop open, he started typing without speaking to me. Without realizing it, my legs started bobbing up and down rapidly like a jackhammer. I consciously tried to stop it by putting my hand on my lap and pressing down.

"Is my neighbor Betty okay?" She was the only other person I could think of. That's how little social connection I had at this point.

"Far as I know," he said casually. Each key stroke he took, I inched a bit closer in my seat, trying to peek at what he was doing.

I tried to think of anyone else but drew a blank. This was my first time ever seeing Hank without Kelly. What if he was lying to me? What if he isn't who he says he is? *Fuck, fuck, fuck,* I cursed myself for being so stupid. How could I let this man into my house who I barely knew?

While he was typing, I reached into my pocket to pull out my phone and dialed Kelly. "Hey... what's up?" At the sound of her voice, calm and casual, though a bit tired, brought a rush of relief.

"Just saying hi. I've got Hank here, he wants to show me something."

"Oh? Yeah, he texted me that he had something to show me too, but I just saw it. Should I come now?"

I looked at Hank and he lifted his shoulders and nodded his head as if to say, "Sure, why not."

"Yeah, that works."

I still didn't know how I felt about Kelly, but I didn't want to be alone with someone I had only met a few times.

He turned the laptop around. And my eyes scanned the screen, trying to process what I was seeing.

"What is this?" I kept scanning. "Is this a Goddamn joke?" I pushed the laptop away.

Hank slowly shook his head side to side and I pulled the laptop back towards me. Like a car crash, I wanted to look but knew it was not good. I was looking for any sign to prove that this wasn't real.

Hank took back the computer and typed in more information, bringing up some back-end data. The IP address was the same as the one he was currently using—so what I'm looking at was created in my home. He showed that it was written in early March of last year, several days before Ian died. Everything matched up for this to be real, and I had no idea how to reconcile anything in my life right now. The only thing I knew for sure was I was alive but I don't know if I wanted to be anymore.

My husband had a blog that he never told me about.

It had one single post.

That he set to publish today, the anniversary of his death.

Forty-Six

And then there was just you
Dedication: To my lovely wife

To my dearest Brittany, you were always the one.

The one I knew I had to be with, to marry, to see this thing to the end.

My name is Ian Foster, and first I want to apologize. I'm not a writer. I'm a business man, a coffee guy.

But I wanted to write a story, so I'm going to give it a shot here. It has all the things people love about a story—love, deception, revenge, and death. Lots of death.

There was a young boy, who grew up in Jersey City, with his mom. His dad had left him when he was very young, rarely visiting. His father lived somewhere in a perfect town in South Jersey with his new, perfect, family. His dad had a lovely wife and a daughter he adored. Sometimes he would come to visit the boy, but not nearly as much as the boy would like. Because his dad liked

It where he was, with the perfect family, his wife and his daughter, Anna.

So, the boy felt left out and unloved. His mom tried her hardest but was barely scraping by, because the boy's father didn't send much money. Sure, he had money, good money, but it went towards the big house, the trophy wife, a fancy blue convertible and making sure Anna feels like a princess.

When the trophy wife got sick, his father came less and less. Always making excuses about needing to take care of her. But who would take care of the boy?

Then one day, the boy was pulled out of class. It was gym class and he remembers being angry, because he was about to win the middle school kickball tournament. His father called to tell him that Anna had died yesterday. He listened to his father tell him through loud sobs how she was biking with a friend too close to the road. She stumbled off the bike and was hit. She was killed instantly.

He thinks his dad sounds like a bit of a baby because he's never heard a grown man cry. In the back of his mind, he wonders if this means his dad will visit more and that part makes him smile a bit.

"I'm sorry, Dad," he said, while picturing his dad picking him up and taking him to a Phillies game. All the kids in his grade liked the Yankees, but he liked the Phillies because his dad did.

Anna's mom was sick, so she passed away a month later. Without her daughter there to tether her to this Earth, she wanted to leave it. The boy hoped the dad would ask him and his

MOM TO LIVE WITH HIM IN THE BIG HOUSE, IN THE NICE TOWN, SO THEY COULD BE A FAMILY AGAIN. THE BOY HAD ALWAYS BEEN TOLD HIS DAD COULDN'T VISIT BECAUSE HIS WIFE WAS SICK, BUT SHE WAS GONE NOW AND HE STILL WASN'T VISITING.

THE BOY COULDN'T UNDERSTAND WHY AND HE CALLED HIS FATHER OVER AND OVER, LEAVING A MESSAGE ON HIS ANSWERING MACHINE, "DAD, WHEN CAN I SEE YOU NEXT?" BUT HE NEVER CALLED BACK AGAIN. HIS MOTHER SAT HIM DOWN ONE DAY.

SHE SAID, "I'M SO SORRY BUT YOUR DAD IS GONE."

"GONE WHERE?" HE ASKED HER.

"HEAVEN," WAS ALL SHE SAID.

"BUT WHY? WHAT HAPPENED?" IT MADE NO SENSE TO THE BOY. HIS DAD WAS SO YOUNG AND HEALTHY.

"SOMETIMES LIFE CAN GIVE YOU MORE THAN YOU CAN HANDLE. YOUR DAD WAS SO OVERCOME BY GRIEF. YOU KNOW HE HAS BEEN THROUGH A LOT WITH THE PASSING OF HIS WIFE AND CHILD."

"MY SISTER," HE CORRECTED HER.

"RIGHT. I KNOW YOU LOVED HIM AND WILL MISS HIM BUT YOU'LL MEET HIM AGAIN IN HEAVEN SOME DAY." HE TOOK HIS OWN LIFE, NEVER EVEN SAYING GOODBYE OR I LOVE YOU TO THE BOY.

SO, THE BOY HAD LOST A LOT OF FAMILY AT THAT POINT. YOU'D THINK THE WORLD WOULD SAY, 'THAT'S ENOUGH, THIS LITTLE BOY CAN'T HANDLE ANYMORE'. BUT THAT ISN'T HOW THINGS WORKED OUT.

HIS MOTHER, WHO LOVED HIM, GOT MIXED UP IN THINGS SHE SHOULDN'T HAVE. THE LOSS OF CHILD SUPPORT MEANT THEY STRUGGLED EVEN MORE. IT ADDED SO MUCH STRESS TO HER LIFE, AND WHEN SHE GOT STRESSED, SHE TURNED MORE TO THE THINGS SHE SHOULDN'T BE DOING. ONE NIGHT, SHE TOOK TOO MANY OF THOSE THINGS, AND HE FOUND HER LAYING ON THE

BATHROOM FLOOR. SHE WAS COLD TO THE TOUCH BUT THE BOY HAD HOPED SHE WOULD WAKE UP. BECAUSE IF SHE DIDN'T, WHO WOULD TAKE CARE OF HIM?

HE LAY WITH HER FOR AN HOUR, SO YOUNG THAT HE JUST THOUGHT IF HE WISHED HARD ENOUGH, SHE'D WAKE UP. BUT OF COURSE SHE DIDN'T. SHE HADN'T SAID GOODBYE EITHER.

THE BOY WAS SENT TO HIS GRANDMOTHER'S HOUSE. SHE TOOK CARE OF HIM THE BEST SHE COULD, BUT SHE WAS VERY OLD. SHE PASSED AWAY WHEN HE WAS EIGHTEEN, CONSIDERED AN ADULT BUT STILL SO YOUNG.

HE HAD NO FAMILY, WITH NO ONE TO CARE FOR HIM AND NO SAFETY NET. HE HAD NO DIRECTION—EXCEPT ONE GOAL. TO GET BACK AT THE GIRL WHO TOOK EVERYTHING FROM HIM. HE WOULD DO THE SAME TO HER. ONE BY ONE, TAKING THE PEOPLE SHE LOVED AND NOT GIVING THEM A CHANCE TO SAY GOODBYE.

SO, THE BOY GREW INTO A MAN HELLBENT ON REVENGE.

HE MET WITH THE CARELESS GIRL, WHO WAS NOW A WOMAN. SHE WAS BEAUTIFUL AND SEEMED TO BE GETTING HER LIFE TOGETHER—UNLIKE HIM, WHO APPEARED SUCCESSFUL BUT WAS CHASING A CURE FOR CHILDHOOD TRAUMA. BUT HE COULD TELL BENEATH IT ALL, SHE WAS DAMAGED.

HER NAME WAS BRITTANY. HE WORKED HIS WAY INTO BRITTANY'S LIFE. ON THE FIRST DATE, HE SAID TO HER, "TELL ME ABOUT YOUR FRIENDS?" AND THE WOMAN REACTED SO TOUCHED BY THIS QUESTION AS IF HER PAST DATES HADN'T SHOWN GENUINE INTEREST IN HER.

"NO ONE HAS EVER ASKED ME THAT ON A DATE BEFORE! YOU SEEM LIKE SUCH A NICE GUY," SHE SAID WITH A BRIGHT SMILE. "MY BEST FRIEND IS NAMED KATIE," SHE STARTED. AND SHE WENT ON AND ON. EACH

DETAIL SHE GAVE, HE TOOK A MENTAL NOTE. IT WAS RATHER EASY FOR THE MAN TO FIND HER FRIEND. THE FACT THAT THEY WERE ON THE PHONE TOGETHER WHEN HE DID IT AND THE FACT THAT SHE HAD TO HEAR IT ALL MADE IT EVEN MORE SATISFYING.

HER GRIEF MADE IT EASIER FOR HIM TO WORK HIS WAY INTO HER LIFE. HE PRETENDED TO BE EVERYTHING SHE NEEDED AT THAT MOMENT BY GIVING HER COMFORT, A SHOULDER TO CRY ON AND A LISTENING EAR.

BY THE NEXT YEAR, THEY WERE DATING EXCLUSIVELY.

THIS ONE, HE DID FROM AFAR, SO SHE WOULD NEVER BE SUSPICIOUS OF HIM. THE WOMAN WAS EXTREMELY CLOSE WITH HER FATHER. HER MOTHER, NOT SO MUCH, THOUGH SHE NEVER WOULD SAY WHY. SHE LOVED HER BUT ALWAYS KEPT HER AT A DISTANCE. SO, IT DIDN'T TAKE MUCH DIGGING TO KNOW WHO WOULD BE NEXT. THE NIGHT BEFORE, HE TAMPERED WITH THEIR CAR. HE KNEW THEY WERE GOING TO MAKE THE DRIVE TO BE WITH HER ON THIS DAY, TO COMFORT HER ON THE ANNIVERSARY OF HER FRIEND'S DEATH. THEIR CAR SWERVED OFF THE ROAD AND THEY BOTH PASSED AWAY. SO FAR, HIS PLAN WAS WORKING PERFECTLY.

THE NEXT YEAR, HE DIDN'T WANT HER TO GET ANY SUSPICIONS. HE STILL WANTED HER TO THINK THAT THIS WAS ALL IN HER HEAD. HE TOLD HER THAT IT WAS ALL A COINCIDENCE, SAYING IT SO OFTEN UNTIL SHE THOUGHT IT HAD TO BE TRUE.

THIS TIME HE PICKED SOMEONE MORE REMOVED FROM THE SITUATION, BUT AT THE SAME TIME IT WAS ALSO THE PERFECT PICK. WHILE SHE SLEPT, HE SNUCK OUT OF THE HOUSE RIGHT AFTER MIDNIGHT. HE WENT TO THE HOME OF HER CHILDHOOD FRIEND AND TOOK HER LIFE. THIS FILLED THE WOMAN WITH GUILT AND grief. She was starting to feel like anyone connected to her might die. It was exactly what he wanted.

The next year, the goal was to take out her sister. This one was a bit more complicated for the man because she didn't like to let him out of her sight. He knew his sister-in-law's routines pretty well at this point. He and his wife drove behind her to make sure she got home okay, completely unaware that he would be the reason harm would come to her. He asked to use her bathroom and slipped into her bedroom. While in there, he added a deadly cocktail of substances to her glass of water that she kept on her nightstand. Before seeing himself out, he planted some pill bottles in her room. He wished his sister-in-law a goodnight and then headed back home with his wife.

And the final year, he was the only one left. She had no one in the world except him. She loved him deeply, so removing himself from the situation would be the most gratifying. With him gone, she'd be left with death after death and no one to provide any comfort. And you think maybe he wouldn't be okay with this, because it's his own life, but you'd be wrong. He was eager to leave this life behind, with all its pain and suffering.

So, while out with his dog, he took a handful of pills and waited for them to make him drowsy. He laid down in the river and without regret, let death take him. It took away the last person the woman had in the entire world. Now, like when he was a little boy, she had no one left to love or to love her.

He thought about taking the dog, so she didn't even have that small comfort, but even he wasn't that evil. Plus, he knew she didn't care for their pet, and he really did love the dog.

The last part of the plan was to give her breadcrumbs so she knew this was intentional, that it was revenge. It would be the final blow to her.

Before his death, he contacted someone from his past, a woman who had always been enamored with him. He knew with one phone call she'd do anything. He buttered her up, which wasn't very difficult, and made her feel special. She was eager to see him and when they met, she seemed desperate for his attention. At that point, he realized he could get her to do pretty much anything. So, he told her to hold on to some of his items. To keep them a secret, unless something should happen to him. Then she should give it to his wife.

He reveled in the fact that opening that box would bring back the memory of what had started all this into motion. He hoped she would see the toy she stole, and the shock would send her into madness. He hoped that on this day, she'd still be looking over her shoulder, fearing that someone else near her might die.

You were always the one who caused me pain. You were always the one who needed to pay.

FORTY-SEVEN

Just then the doorbell rang, and Hank must have let Kelly in. I was in a daze. Reading his story consumed me so much that I had blocked out the world around me. After reading the final line, I heard Kelly exhale followed by, "God. Damn." Then she looked at me, trying to read my face for any expression so she could figure out what to say to me. But my facial expression was devoid of any emotion. My brain couldn't figure out what I just read, let alone figure out what this meant for my whole life.

I cleared my throat and said, "Guys, I think I need a moment."

They nodded without saying anything. I saw him take the laptop, already re-reading the blog post. I sprinted to my room, surprised my legs could even carry me at this point. I locked the door and then collapsed on the bed like a house of cards meeting a gust of wind. I was trying to process the significance of Ian's final message.

I took Mable out of the bassinet and sat beside Rosco, bringing everyone I loved as close to me as possible.

The man I loved, who I was sure loved me to the ends of the Earth and back, didn't love me at all. In fact, he let a deep hatred and resentment stew in him for decades. His goal was to take everything from me, to leave me as empty as he was all those years. But he didn't know that he hadn't taken everyone from me. In fact, he had given me the greatest love of my life, our daughter.

For her sake, I needed to remain strong. I couldn't let this shred me to pieces because my daughter deserves a present and loving mother. I took deep breaths, talking to myself on each inhale and exhale while I stroked the soft brown hair on top of her head.

"You can get up and continue on."

"Your daughter needs you."

"You've handled so much already; you can handle this." Each phrase I said to myself calmed me bit by bit.

When I reemerged from the room with Mable in my arms and Rosco in tow, they looked up, surprised to see me so soon. I looked down at the perfect child in my arms. When she opened her eyes, I was filled with hope—for her, for our future.

"Can we do anything? Help you in any way?"

"Yeah. We need to tell my story. Clear my name. And shut this book so I can start a new one."

"Are you sure? I totally understand if you aren't ready. You and your daughter need to be the priority," she said.

"I actually think I need this more than anything."

"Okay. Okay. If you really think that's what will be good for you."

I nodded, knowing that this finally was the right choice. I had been wavering before, knowing that the terror was still out there. But now that I knew for sure I'd be safe, telling my story would be therapeutic.

Kelly and I arranged to meet the next day.

After they left, I put Mable on her play mat. I logged onto my own device and read the post again while occasionally moving the brightly colored toys that hung above her head. At the bottom there was a response section. I began to type to my dead husband, my tormentor. I wrote, letting every emotion pour out of my heart but didn't hit send. I just let the letter hang there, unsure if I would ever send it. Either way, it felt good to address him with my final thoughts.

FORTY-EIGHT

After reading Ian's blog post, it changed my perception of Kelly. There were days when I was suspicious of her behavior but now, I understood that she was just a bit misguided in her effort to develop the podcast and that led her to some inconsiderate statements. We actually ended up talking about it, and I let her know my feelings, and she apologized. We were in a good place when we started to meet again that final week.

Kelly ended up tossing all the previous recordings. I was hiding most of myself, and it could be heard in my evasive responses, my lack of emotion.

For seven days of recording, each tragedy that I spoke of alleviated some of the pain and guilt. For once, I held nothing back. My emotions were raw. I don't know what she would and wouldn't use, but it was so healing to be able to tell my story.

I leaned in close to the microphone, knowing this would close this chapter of my life. Kelly had adapted to her podcaster voice as she began: "So today, we have joining us for our final session, Brittany Foster. So, let's start off with, how are you doing?"

"All things considered I'm getting by. But I'm actually no

longer Brittany Foster. I'm in the process of switching back to my maiden name, and I'm going by that now."

She asked me the questions we'd been going over and over. I'd told this so many times, and I promised that after today, I'd never speak of it again, with one exception. If my daughter ever asked, I'd tell her.

Once we reached the end of the standard questions, she asked, "What's life like today for you?"

"It's hard to put into words. I try, for my daughter's sake, to be as mentally healthy as possible, but those traumas never fully leave you. And trauma shapes how you move in the world and how you react to it. Every action I take, every word I speak, it looms in the background, shadowing over it all."

I took in a deep breathe before continuing, "I know I'll never date again, so I'm forever a single mom without a support system. I try, for her sake, to not let those traumas affect how I parent, but I'm sure I'm more of a helicopter parent that I would have been."

"I'm positive our audience wants to see you thrive. Other than your daughter, what are some of the positive things in your life?"

I paused for a second, getting a bit choked up. "Many things actually. My dog Rosco, of course. I got a new job in social media marketing. My daughter and I moved into a small house in a new town. I'm most thankful that I am able to hold on to the good memories of my loved ones, and share those stories with my daughter. My daughter and I laugh together, and I cherish those carefree moments. Each morning, I wake to see the sunrise, and it's the most beautiful thing because it's proof that I get another day and there's nothing more of a blessing than getting another day."

She ended with one final question, "What do you want everyone to know about you now?"

I sucked in a breath and paused to ponder the question. This will be the last thing listeners hear from me and from the podcast. I wanted to be careful with my words.

"I want people to know..." *What do I want them to know*

about me? About this situation? About my future? I looked up at Kelly and all the previous frustrations were gone. She waited patiently for me to formulate my answers and then gave me an encouraging smile.

I started again when I composed my thoughts. "I want people to know that you are stronger than you think you are. That no matter what life throws at you, you just somehow find it in you to keep going." She was nodding in agreement so I continued, "And I want them to know that all the loss I have in my life does not mean that I've lost love. I still have all the love and memories of those who have passed and I keep those with me each day. And that I feel blessed to have my daughter."

And with that, she stopped the recording, and my story had been told.

With no more words spoken between us, I felt a twinge of sadness. I'd never been good at saying goodbye or knowing things are going to end. Kelly walked around the table, and I stood up to embrace her.

She whispered into my ear, "You are the bravest woman I know, and you deserve all the sunrises."

I nodded, still embracing her, thankful for this day.

Knowing that I don't truly deserve it.

FORTY-NINE

It is the first March 13th in years since I have felt a sense of peace. This day still harbors so much negative emotion but the anxiety is gone, and someday there will be acceptance.

The podcast came out, and Kelly told me it was a big success. I never bothered looking at the reviews because I knew there would be things said that would crush me. I turned down offers to come on local radio stations and even one TV spot. I put myself out there with the podcast. I wanted my story to be heard so I could clear my name. But that was it for me. I won't talk about it anymore.

So, when people call for quotes for their articles, I just tell them I'm focusing on my daughter and then say goodbye.

Mable has a full head of brown hair, the same shade as mine, now that I've let the natural color return. I'm no longer hiding myself from the world. Her hair is long enough that I can put it into a little ponytail. She is starting to walk and I watch her teeter around the living room, grasping for nearby objects to steady herself. For now, she's oblivious to the chaos that surrounded her while she was growing inside of me and the fear I had when she came into the world.

Now all is calm, and I'll keep it that way for her for as long as possible. Sure, she will hear things when she is older. I can't avoid that. But where we stand today, things are good.

As I watch her sleep during her mid-day nap, I grab the laptop, thankful for a few moments of rest. I open the web browsers and see there are way too many tabs open. I start to delete them one by one until all that is left is Ian's blog page which I have had open for exactly one year today. My response is still on the page, unsent. I read it over one more time.

To Ian:

There was so much I wanted to share with you. I thought we had our whole lives ahead for us to grow together, start a family, travel the world.

I know I should harbor so much anger toward you for all that you've done, but all I can think of is this hurt little boy struggling to find a place in the world. It must have been excruciating. Some messed up part of me wishes I could go back, and help that little boy, show him that he is very loved, and maybe all this could have been different.

And based on what I did, what I took from you, I can almost accept what you did in return.

Anna's death wasn't an accident. Maybe you felt that all along.

I intentionally pushed her. I want to say that it was the impulsivity of a broken child but I know that isn't true. I did it so her dad would hurt like I had been hurting.

So, it looks like we have more in common than you'll ever know, my love.

I press delete on the love letter that will live in my heart forever.

Dear reader,

Thank you for taking a chance on my independently published book! If you enjoyed this book, please spread the word. Tell a friend, suggest it be your book club's next pick, leave a review and post this book on your social media sites.

If you are interested in following my writing journey, including my next book coming Fall 2026, please use the QR code to follow me.

Can't wait to share the next book with you.

Best,

A.L.L.

About the Author

Amber lives in New Jersey with her family. She has published 4 books. In addition to writing, she enjoys travel, finding new coffee shops, running and journaling.

www.ingramcontent.com/pod-product-compliance
Lightning Source LLC
Chambersburg PA
CBHW030912060726
47591CB00005B/1516